RETURN OF THE SHADOWS

RETURN OF THE SHADOWS

Book Four Breaking the Spell

DONALD L MARINO

Author's Ink

Copyright © 2023 by Donald Marino

All rights reserved. No part of this book may be reproduced in any manner whatsoever without written permission except in the case of brief quotations embodied in critical articles and reviews.

First Printing, 2023

Prologue

The Goddess Atla, was shining brightly, as she floated around the lake of souls that separated her realm from that of her sisters. The lake held those souls that just passed. The souls that when they were mortal never believed in either Goddess. The souls that were now lost and needed guidance to move on. The lake had great contrast. The Goddess Atla side was all light, plants and flowers were always blooming. Warmth was felt in every corner of her side of the lake. It made you smile and take deep breaths to get every beautiful scent. The Goddess Hel's side was all dead, nothing grew there, the air was very heavy making it very hard to breathe.

The Goddess Atla looked at the lake and felt the grief of those who were there. They seemed to reach out to her now, pleading for help. She watched small bright lights trying to help them to accept the Goddess Atla, but there were also the dark lights, the shadows. They were working for her sister. Too many souls had followed them to her sisters' side and soon regretted it. It had been this way for many millennia.

"You were always the soft one." The Goddess Hel's voice came as she came out of the shadows from her side of the lake. Her dark presents sent light fleeing, except for the light around Atla.

"And you the cold hearted one." The Goddess Atla said and felt bad for saying so.

"I love when my darkness rubs off on you." The Goddess Hel said. Loving that she got Atla to make a negative comment.

"Why are you here? This is my time at the lake." The Goddess Atla said.

Each Goddess had their own time at the lake. They could help bring souls to their side, and they we're not supposed to interrupt each other. Their father had set that up and it was a rule to never be broken.

"Are you going to tell daddy?" The Goddess Hel was smug.

"No." The Goddess Atla said as she turned back to the lake.

"I thought maybe we could have some sister bonding time."

The Goddess Atla turned and looked at her, then turned back to the lake.

"You never spend time with me." The Goddess Hel said as she moved closer.

"That is close enough. This is my side of the lake, and no darkness is allowed." The Goddess Atla scolded her as she moved toward the center of her side of the lake.

"That isn't very nice. I am trying to make amends with you."

"I would like to believe you, but you are not to be trusted." The Goddess Atla said as she moved closer to the lake and two souls flew out and into the light. She smiled to herself.

"Looks like you got a couple of souls." The Goddess Hel said trying to sound happy, but not doing a good job of it.

"More like I saved two souls. Now why don't you move along and let me have my time." The Goddess Atla said as she looked back into the lake.

"That hurts." The Goddess Hel said trying again to sound sincere, but not pulling it off.

"What is it you want?" The Goddess Atla finally asked. "I know it's not to have sister time."

"Why are you so distrusting of me?"

"Experience tells me to."

The Goddess Hel moved closer again.

"Stop, I said no darkness on my side of the lake."

"This isn't your side." The Goddess Hel growled now.

"What?" The Goddess Atla was confused, and suddenly she saw the Goddess Hel had put a spell on the lake. She was now standing in the middle of the Goddess Hel's side. She had let her sister trick her, now she was stuck where she should not be. The darkness surrounded her, she tried to fight it off, but she was soon overwhelmed and felt sick to her soul.

"Shadows trap her now. Now you are mine." She said as she approached her. She cast as spell and there was a cage of darkness surrounding the Goddess Atla. The Shadows move the cage into the darkness.

"Not to worry my sister. I will take care of those who worship you." She laughed as she followed the cage.

A few minutes later Lor's soul was by the lake.

Chapter One

"He is down here." Arastrude yelled back to Dagrel. She walked up to O, who was sitting by the Creek that ran through their property. They went looking for him after he missed breakfast. This was his favorite place to sit when he was thinking. O loved the sound of the water rushing over the rocks. It was early fall, and leaves were starting to change on the trees along the banks. Several had already fallen and were floating down the creek. The small animals of the woods were preparing for winter.

Arastrude, Dagrel and O had moved into a farm just south of the Dwarf capital city. The council had given it to them after the balance was restored as a thank you. That was seventy years ago now, and Arastrude had kept her promise to the Goddess Atla to take care of O. Her and Dagrel had several children and they had grown and moved off on their own now, but they still had O.

"What is wrong?" Arastrude ask as she sat beside him.

"O not know. O asked pretty lady for help, but she not talk to O." O said in his child like way, as he sighed heavily.

"O what's going on buddy?" Dagrel asked as he sat down on the other side of O.

"O made pretty lady mad, and now she not help O." O said with tears in his eyes.

"No, I'm sure that's not true." Dagrel said as he looked to Arastrude for help.

"O bad troll?" O asked Arastrude

"No, No, O you are a very good troll." Arastrude assured him

"What is it you need help with my friend?" Dagrel asked

"O have dream, not understand."

"What dream?" Arastrude asked

"Friend need help."

"What Friend?" Dagrel asked

"Alastrine."

"Alastrine." Arastrude and Dagrel said together.

"Yes." O looked back and forth at both.

"Then we will go see him, maybe he can tell us why the Goddess isn't around right now." Dagrel said

"Really!" O was excited.

"Yes, we will leave this afternoon."

"O go pack." O stood, smiling.

"Yes, O go pack. I will get the boys to help me here." Arastrude said.

O got up and went to his room in the barn.

"There is a problem." Arastrude said

"What is that?"

"The Goddess isn't answering me either."

"What are you talking about?" Dagrel was confused.

"I'm having dreams. Whiley came to me. Said beware it's been found."

"What!?"

"It happened last night for the third time. Today for the second time I went to my safe place and the Goddess didn't answer me." Arastrude said showing concern in her face.

"What do you think it means?"

"I thought maybe my dreams were nothing to worry about, and that is why the Goddess didn't come."

"And now?"

"Now, with O's problems, and other things I am noticing." Arastrude stopped and sighed.

"Other stuff?"

"Yes. Did you notice how fast the leaves are changing?"

"It may be a little early."

"It's very early, and the crops seem to have stopped growing like they were."

"Are you sure?"

"Yes, you know I have a close connection to the earth ever since I used the stone. I'm telling you something is wrong."

"Do you want to go with us? The boys can handle…"

"No, I want to go to the elders and see if they have any insight."

"That's a very good idea." He said as he looked into her eyes and saw concern that he hadn't seen in a very long time. "I'm sure it's nothing to worry about." He said as he hugged her.

"I hope you are right. Go pack, the sooner we figure this out the better."

"May the Goddess bless us." She added as He walked away.

"May the Goddess always bless us." He said Looking back at her and smiled.

* * * * *

Edo jerked himself awake again. Edo was the son of Ren, the second son of Lor. Lor had always overlooked Ren when he was younger in favor of his older brother Rex. After the war, with everything that his father had done, Ren and his mother didn't go back to the island. They stayed in the countryside just outside of Juna. Even though they disowned Lor, a lot of hawk people still looked down on them. They wanted to distance themselves as far from trouble as they could. Alastrine over the years had checked in on them. He assured them that Lor had been tricked by the Goddess Hel, and that Lor's decisions were his own and they were not responsible. That did little for his mother who never got over Lor's turning on the four races and killing their son. A memorial had been built to Rex, without whom Lor may not have been defeated.

Edo, looked like a young Lor, with black beak, light brown hair and green eyes. He now sat on his bed. He had been having dreams of Lor, where he keeps asking for his help. He hadn't said anything to anyone because mentioning Lor's name had been forbidden. Now he looked on his nightstand and a book laid there that he had not put there. He picked it up and opened it slowly. As he read the pages, he couldn't believe what it was. It was a diary that Lor had kept when he was Edo's age. A knock came at his door, and he quickly put the book under his pillow.

"Sleepy head are you going to eat breakfast?" Jen, his mother, asked.

"Yes, mom. I'll be down in a minute." Edo said slowly, his mind still reeling.

"Ok, cause if you are going to the island today you should get an early start." Jen said as her voice trailed off down the hall.

Edo was going to the island today to meet with his cousin, who said he had work for him. He packed a bag since he wasn't sure how long he was going to be there. He was happy about that. He hoped the dream wouldn't follow him there. He looked back at his pillow, as he was about to leave his room, went and grabbed the book and put it into his bag. He didn't want his mother or grandmother to find it if they decided to clean his room, while he was gone. He had no idea where it came from but didn't want to have to explain it. He left his room and went to eat breakfast.

"You ok dear, not like you to sleep so late." Jen said as he sat down.

He looked around his father wasn't there.

"He headed out for the day already." Jen answered his question before he asked it.

"I guess I did sleep late." Edo said as he started eating.

"Yes, you did." Jen looked at him and smiled. Edo was her only child. She almost died giving birth to him and was unable to bear any more children.

"I didn't sleep really well, guess I'm excited about going to the island today." He lied.

"Yes, please be careful there. Stay with your cousin." She warned him.

"I know." He smiled. He loved how protective she was of him, but sometimes it was over kill.

"Well, you know most still haven't forgotten, and you know you look." She stopped short of saying his name.

"Yes, I know mom." He smiled at her.

"I just worry is all." She leaned over and kissed him lightly on the forehead.

"I will be safe mom. I need to get going, I'm already running late." He stood and hugged Jen and kissed her on the cheek. "I love you mom. I will take care and I will see you soon." he turned and headed out the door.

Chapter Two

Alastrine walked out of his house deep in thought. For the fifth time this week he meditated and went to his safe place looking to talk to the Goddess. For the fifth time she didn't show. There was nothing of importance that he needed, but he liked to meet with her. He always felt recharged after doing so. Alastrine took a deep breath stopped and looked around.

"Oh Alastrine, there you are." Mary Jean said as she walked up to him.

Mary Jean was the Governor of Moray. She had black hair, brown eyes, small framed and only five foot three. She was the daughter of Sara, who was the daughter of Alex and Sherry. Sara had become governor after Alex retired, and now Mary Jean had followed her mother's footsteps. Where Sara was a strong leader, Mary Jean was not. Mary Jean had problems making decisions, often wanting Alastrine to tell her what to do.

"Yes Mary Jean. How are you?" Alastrine said as he snapped back to reality.

"The council is meeting. They are talking about the trade route." Mary Jean looked at Alastrine.

"And what is it you want?" Alastrine asked knowing what it was already.

"Well, I'm not sure what I should do."

"I see."

"What do you think?" Mary Jean asked sheepishly

"Does it matter?"

"Well.."

"You know what is good and what is not. You don't need my help."

"I know."

"Is there anything else you need?"

"No, I guess not."

"Mary Jean. You are bright and know what to do. Stop worrying about what people think. If you do the right thing, the ones that matter will be happy."

"You're right."

"OK, I have some things I need to do." He said as he started to walk away.

"Ok, so then I should vote in favor."

"I have issues to tend to as do you. I have great faith in you." He turned back and kissed her on the forehead, then walked away.

As Alastrine walked, he felt bad for Mary Jean, she was so scared to make a decision it almost totally crippled her. Alastrine's thoughts soon went back to his issues, and the smell was back that had caught his attention before Mary Jean stopped him. It's the smell of fall in the air, but it was too early for that. Summer was ending, but fall was just starting and the air shouldn't have such a crisp smell. As Alastrine looked up a leaf fell from a tree and floated to the ground in front of him.

"It is way too early for this." Alastrine said as he picked up the leaf. "I think it is time I visit the elf king." Alastrine turned and went back to his house to pack.

* * * *

Ayre walked out into the garden. Fall was coming and he loved the smell in the air. Although he was confused to see leaves turning already.

"It is strange isn't it." Ryo said as he entered the garden.

Ayre turned and smiled at seeing his old friend. "It's been a while since you have come to see me. What brings you by?"

"What you were just thinking. That is what has brought me by." Ryo said looking back at the trees.

"It's an early fall." Ayre said without much concern.

"It's way too early. Something is off."

"Are you sure it isn't you who are off. How old are you now?"

"My age has everything to do with this, as a matter of fact."

"Really, how so?"

"In over five hundred years I have never seen a fall this early. That is what makes me think something is wrong."

"Well, you may have a point. Shall we meditate and talk to the Goddess?"

"That's a great idea, except I have already tried that and got nothing."

"What are you saying?" He was concerned to hear the Goddess didn't answer.

"I have tried for several days now; the Goddess has not answered me. That is why I have come to talk to you."

"I have not tried to talk to the Goddess in several days. I was going to meditate in the garden today."

"I have a feeling we are going to get visitors."

"Alastrine?"

"Among others I suspect. If the Goddess is not answering they will come here for help. We have use of the only other magic."

"Not true. There are many witches out their practicing. Maybe they could offer some help or answers as well."

"That's not a bad idea. We could send scouts to find them and ask for help, but that will take a lot of time we may not have."

"What are you talking about?"

"Fall is coming fast. The crops are not ready yet, but if fall sets in it will kill the crops before we can harvest them. It will be a long winter with very little food."

"I hadn't thought about that."

"I don't think we were supposed to think about it."

"What are you suggesting?"

"I think she is behind everything that is happening. She has a new plan to destroy us and we need to figure it out before she completes it."

"She?" Ayre said and knew Ryo was talking about the Goddess Hel by the look in his eyes. Ayre's heart sank. It hadn't been that long ago that they had beat her and now they may have to fight her again. He wasn't looking forward to that. "What do you suppose she has already done?"

"If she had somehow done something to the Goddess Atla, she could do whatever she wants to do."

"And that's why the Goddess isn't answering."

"I'm afraid that is what I believe is going on. Why she chose now to do it I have not figured out yet. I am sure we will soon find out."

"Am I glad I found you two." They both turned to see Felix before them.

"What is it?" Ayre asked.

"We have problems."

Chapter Three

Under the city of Vwnrush, in a small room a woman with black hair, brown eyes and dark skin was reading a book. It was a book she had pulled from a bookshelf, that was a secret door. The books once belonged to Katie and had been handed down. Lynn who was now looking through the books was the granddaughter of Katie. Katie and Nonmumi had adopted a young girl, April, after the war was over and Lynn was the daughter of April. Lynn had picked up magic very easily and loved it. Lynn now was looking through books to see if the things she noticed happening had ever happen before.

"I don't understand. There is nothing here to help me at all." She said frustrated as she closed another book.

She pulled out a Cauldron and filled it with water. Then added herbs as she chanted some words and the water started to stir.

"Now let's see what I can see." She said as images in the swirling waters started to become clear.

"O and Dagrel what are they doing?" She said as an image of them walking with packs appeared. "Are they coming this way?" She blinked her eyes not believing what she was seeing. "Dagrel is really going to bring a troll to the city?"

The image disappeared and other images swirled around. Lynn squinted her eyes to try and pull an image forward. The elf king came up. He looked confused. There were several others with him, but she was unclear who they were. The elf king kept looking at leaves falling around him.

"The early fall that I am seeing. The elf king is seeing it to." She said happy to see someone else was seeing it.

The images swirled again and again she squinted her brown eyes to try and pull up an image. A diary came up.

"Whose diary is this, does it have the answers I need?" She said as she looked at the image. "Please Goddess show me more."

Suddenly there were shadows in front of her. They were trying to pull her in. She stepped back shocked that the shadows were able to get to her.

"The Goddess protects me here; how did that happen?" She said as she closed the spell.

She paced back and forth. Pulled several more books and looked for the diary she saw.

"Ok, I know O and Dagrel must be looking for help, to come to the city. The elf king knows something is wrong and whoever is with him must be asking questions." She said as she started to pace again.

"I will go intercept O and Dagrel, we will go see the elf king. If answers are going to be found, the elf king will find them." She said as she turned and opened the bookcase door and left.

* * * *

As Edo flew his thoughts drifted, wondering anew how he got the diary and why. The flight seemed to go by fast, as he soon landed on the north side of the island. He was supposed to meet his cousin Alex at the fish market. He walked slowly toward the market thinking about asking his cousin if he knew of any diary.

"Edo where are you going?" Alex said as he grabbed Edo's arm.

Edo jumped and looked to see Alex. Alex was medium build with black beak, brown hair and eyes.

"Oh, sorry. I have some things on my mind." Edo said as he shook Alex's hand.

"That's ok, thanks for coming. I am in need of help. I lost six employees in one week. I thought I was going to have to close my stand at the market. That would have ended bad." Alex shook his head.

"No problem. I have been looking to get off the farm anyway."

"Come with me. I will show you where you will be staying and then we will head to the market." Alex smiled and started walking away from the market.

"I am looking forward to being here for a while. I need to be around people. Life on the farm is very lonely. Not my thing." Edo said as they walked.

"I hear you." Alex said as he opened the door of a small house near the foot of a mountain trail. "It's not much but it is home."

'Still the bachelor." Edo laughed as he looked around. The house was tiny. A kitchen and living room combined. A small hall that led to two rooms. The house was untidy, but not dirty.

"You have the room on the left. You can put your things away and I'll meet you at the market." Alex said as he turned to leave.

Edo went to his room and put his clothes in a small dresser. Then he pulled out the diary and staired at it for a few moments. He sighed heavy and put the diary in the draw with his clothes and left.

He got to the stand at the market, and it was very busy. He spent the rest of the day working and had no time to think about the diary or the dreams.

Chapter Four

Mary Jean sat in her office looking at the bill for the proposed trading route. The council had unanimously voted for it. A lot of people in town had said that it might take jobs away from them. One of those people now stood in front of her.

"Mary, if you sign that people will lose here. Jobs will go to Lorn, and our people will lose everything." Oliver said to her.

Oliver was six-foot-tall, slim with black hair and green eyes. Oliver had been in the orphanage that Whiley and Leigh had open after the war. When they both passed away, almost ten years ago, Oliver had taken over and ran it for almost five years before closing it down. Most people say they stopped donating to it because they saw how poorly he was running it. It seemed the donations went to him, not the children. Conditions became so poor that children had run away back to the streets. Oliver somehow managed to get Mary Jeans trust and had become someone she listened to. That did not set well with the Council.

"The council said I will increase jobs." Mary Jean said.

"The council." Oliver laughed. "They are most likely being paid by Lorn's Governor."

"I don't think they." She started.

"Are you sure?" He cut her off.

"Well no." She admitted.

"Let me do some research before you sign it."

"OK." Mary Jean sighed knowing the council was not going to be happy with the delay.

"I will get back to you in a couple of days with what I find out." Oliver said as he left.

Mary Jean waited a few minutes and left her office and went for a walk. As Mary Jean walked toward the east gate, she saw Alastrine walking a horse.

"Where are you going?" Mary Jean asked as she walked up to Alastrine.

"I am going to see the elf king."

"Why?"

He sighed, knowing the concern was more because she was not going to have him to give her answers, that she already knew.

"I have some things I have to discuss with the elf king."

"How long will you be gone?"

"I don't know, I am sure you will be fine."

"I know, I have Oliver."

"Yes, Oliver. Please be careful with him."

"Why?"

"He means well, but he doesn't always make the best decisions."

"OK."

"OK then. I will see you when I get back." Alastrine said as he got on his horse at the gate and rode out with a wave goodbye.

"Ok, have a safe trip and may the goddess bless you." Mary Jean said as she watched him ride off.

* * * * *

Arastrude received word late in the afternoon that the elders would see her right away. This made her worry even more, because the elders never reacted this fast. Arastrude thought it would be a couple of days before she heard from them.

"Elders, thank you for seeing me so fast." She said as she approached the apple tree where they sat.

"My dear, it is our pleasure to see you."

"I'm concerned." Arastrude started.

"And with good reason we feel."

"Fall has come fast. The Goddess has not answered when called upon." Arastrude reported.

"We have had the same problems with regard to the Goddess."

"The Goddess's sister is up to no good we feel." Another elder added.

"Is there anything I can do?"

"My dear you and Dagrel have done so much for the Dwarfs already. We hate to ask more of you."

"But."

"We feel we need to send a contingent to the elf king and get some answers. We feel you should lead this contingent."

"I see."

"The rest of the contingent will be at your house first thing in the morning."

"May the Goddess bless you and the task we have given you." The head elder said, and they all stood and left. Arastrude was left wondering what answers she was going to get and if she would like them.

Chapter Five

Lor's soul lurked around the lake for a while not sure what to do. Lor stayed by the lakes edge.

"I should tell someone what I saw." He said out loud and sighed. "But who?"

Lor had asked the Goddess Atla to forgive him, just before he died, and she did. Therefor Lor's soul went into the light. The problem was everyone knew what he had done, and even though he had been forgiven he knew it was not forgotten.

"Maybe I should tell one of the angels." Lor said thinking out loud. "But which one?"

As Lor was thinking he started to feel weird. Lor looked down and noticed the flowers that had been blooming by him were now dead and black. He felt something move around him.

"Well, well look who it is." A familiar voice said to him and Lor went cold. "You do remember me?" The voice said.

"I do." Lor said without really wanting to.

"Now let's see the last time we were together." The shadow started.

"You nearly destroyed the four races." Lor finished and he started to move away.

The Shadow moved to block his path.

"We. We nearly destroyed the four races." The shadow corrected him.

"I had nothing to do with that."

"You picked up the sword."

"I was tricked into doing that."

"Not how I remember it." The shadows said sailing around Lor killing more of the flowers close by him.

"Listen I don't have to listen to you. I have things I need to do." Lor said and started to move again.

"Like go for help." The shadow laughed.

Lor glared at the shadow and kept moving.

"Don't you miss the feeling of power you had?"

"No." Lor said as he began to meditate to push the shadow away from him.

"You say no, but I'm not convinced."

Lor continued to meditate.

"You can meditate all you want. You and I have a connection that can't be broke." The Shadow hissed at him.

"Your hissing tells me my meditation is working."

"Our connection is strong. How do you think I found you here?"

Lor broke his meditation as that scared him. How had he found him so easily?

"Part of me is still in you."

"No, I pushed you out of me. The Goddess's magic sent you back to where you came from." Lor said trying to control his fear.

"Afraid to say her name?" The Shadow hissed softly now, feeling like he was in control.

"No." Lor said stubbornly.

"Then say it. Call upon her."

"No!" Lor almost yelled now.

"You know you want to feel that power again." The shadow almost ingulfed him now.

"No!" Lor yelled this time.

"She can put us together again. Give us our sword back. Give us life again." The shadow's voice was full of excitement.

"No!" Lor yelled again.

"Father what's going on?" Rex's voice came through.

"Help me." Lor yelled at hearing Rex's voice but not sure where he was.

"Leave." The shadow hissed at him.

"Let my father go! You have no power here." Rex yelled.

A bright light broke through the darkness that had surrounded Lor and he blacked out.

* * * *

A black candle in a dark room was lit. A man kneeled in front of it, with something shiny in front of his knees.

"My lady, I am here." The man said.

"My plans are right on track." The Goddess Hel said.

"What can I do to help my lady?"

"Has Alastrine left the city as I expected him to?"

"Yes, my lady."

"Good, I can sense that the magical items are still in his house."

"What is it you need me to do my lady?"

"I want you to get the magical items Alastrine is guarding."

"How?"

"Take Shadow strike and sneak into Alastrine's house. Shadow strike will take you to where they are hiding, and help you break the spell that protects them."

"What should I do with them then my lady."

"Bring them here and call upon me."

"Ok, my lady anything for you."

"Now go and don't disappoint me."

"Yes, my lady." The man said and the Goddess was gone. He put out the candle and left the room.

Chapter Six

"O scared." O said breaking the silence, they had been walking in ever since they ate lunch.

"Scared of what?" Dagrel asked. Dagrel was scared himself, but wanted to know what scared O.

"Pretty lady not talking to us."

"Yes, I know."

"Why pretty lady mad at us."

"I don't think she is, buddy."

"Did I make her mad?"

"No, I'm sure none of us did."

They walked for a while longer.

"What was your dream?" Dagrel asked.

"Alastrine was looking for something."

"Anything else?"

"He asked for help. Things come after him. Hurt him."

"What was coming after him?"

"O not sure."

"I see."

A few more minutes passed.

"Will Alastrine know why pretty lady mad?" O asked.

"I don't think the pretty." Dagrel started to say then stopped. "I hope so." Dagrel smiled at O.

"Well, there you are." A voice came from the woods.

Dagrel and O both turned ready to fight.

"Why would you scare us like that?" Dagrel said as a dark complected lady walked out. Her black hair was braided and pulled back, her brown eyes smiled at them, and they relaxed at seeing her.

Lynn had met Dagrel, Arastrude and O when she was younger. She hadn't changed her looks much over the years, so Dagrel recognized her.

"Well, I'm not going to lie, it was funny." Lynn smiled at them.

"I will never understand human's sense of humor." Dagrel muttered.

"So, you are taking a troll to the city?" Lynn half laughed.

"O good troll." O started and Dagrel put his hand up to stop him.

"We are on our way to see Alastrine."

"Must be pretty important, you are taking a troll into the human lands."

"For your information." Dagrel stopped and looked at Lynn. "How did you know we were going to be here?"

"How do you think?"

"O not hurt anyone." O said still annoyed at Lynn's statement.

"I know O, but others may not know that, is all I am saying. They would attack first and ask questions later." Lynn said smiling at O.

"So why were you checking on things?" Dagrel asked clearly annoyed at her.

"Why so upset?" Lynn asked.

"I asked first."

"Calm down, we are on the same side."

"Same side?"

"Yes. There is something clearly wrong."

Dagrel and O both just looked at her, waiting for her to say more. O was still hurt by her statement, and Dagrel didn't want to reveal anything to her just yet.

"Ok, fine. The Goddess isn't answering me, so I did a spell to see what was going on." Lynn finally said.

"And you saw us?"

"Among other things. I looked through all my books and there was nothing about the Goddess not responding."

"What other things?"

"Then shadows came through at the end. Shadows in a room that the Goddess protects."

"What other things?"

"I saw the elf king; I think we need to go there."

"We?"

"Yes, I saw you two for a reason and then the elf king. I think that means we should head there."

"You think Alastrine is going to be there?"

"Among others, yes."

Dagrel looked at O then back at Lynn.

"O want to help Alastrine."

"Do you really think Alastrine is going to the elf king?" Dagrel asked.

"It makes sense. The elf king has more history and knowledge than anyone else. If we need answers that is where we would find them."

Dagrel looked at O who shrugged his shoulders.

"O want to help Alastrine." O said again.

"OK fine, we will go with you."

Lynn smiled stepped back into the woods and grabbed a pack she had hidden there.

"Felt pretty sure we would go with you." Dagrel looked at her with a raised eyebrow.

"Always be prepared." Lynn said as she put the pack on her back. "By the way O. I think you are a good troll, and I am looking forward to this trip with you." Lynn said as she started walking.

O smiled and looked at Dagrel. Dagrel sighed.

"You are too easy. Let's go." Dagrel followed after Lynn with O in toe.

* * * *

Lauren woke again sitting straight up in her bed. Sweat was running down her forehead. She brushed her long brown hair back. Lauren could have been Barney's twin, she looked so much like him. Her big brown eyes showed the same compassion her grandfathers did, everyone always commented on her looks. Lauren was the daughter of George and Nancy. George was the son of Barny, who kept his promise and rebuilt Perth. He married Bell, Alex's daughter. Lauren had lived with Barny and Bell most of her life. Her mother passed away in childbirth and George was always away working. But now Barney and Bell both passed several years ago, and she was pretty much on her own.

"What is it you want me to do?" Lauren said as she sat on her bed. She thought about her dream again. Her friend Hunter was in it. Hunter was a boy who lived on the streets and wore rags for clothes. She had often tried to get him to clean up. Hunter always refused; he loved living the way he did.

Lauren got up, got dressed and headed out. Everyone in town knew her, so she spent a lot of time talking to people, always seemed to be running late. That frustrated her, but she was always polite to all that talked to her. Today she wanted to find Hunter and talk to him. She hoped maybe he would know what was going on.

"There you are." Lauren said when she found him almost an hour later by the river fishing.

"I have been here all day." Hunter looked up at her. Hunter was a good six inches taller than her. He was well built from working on local farms to survive. Hunter's dirty blond hair was a mess, as always, and his green eyes made Lauren week in the knees. He smiled at her.

"Yes, I am sure you have." Lauren smiled at him. He always made her smile.

"What is it you need?" Hunter asked her as she sat down beside him.

"I'm not sure." Lauren said unsure of how to bring up her dream.

"Seems like something is on your mind."

"Well, I have been having the same dream for a couple days."

"Want to tell me about it?"

"I do but I'm not sure where to begin."

"The beginning would be a good place to start."

"OK, so grand pa Barney has come to me."

"That seems like a good thing."

"Yes, then I see you and me."

"And?"

"The next thing I see is the elf king."

"OK?"

"That's it. It just keeps repeating."

"Seems like we have a trip in our future."

"What?" Lauren said not expecting that answer.

"He is telling you that we need to go see the elf king." Hunter said as he pulled his line out of the water.

"Are you serious?" Lauren was confused.

"Yes, go pack. It must be important for him to keep coming to you."

"I can't just pick up and go."

"Why not?"

"Well." Lauren couldn't think of a reason.

"OK then. We will leave this afternoon. I will meet you at your house." He started walking away.

"Wait." Lauren said and Hunter turned to look at her.

"What? Listen if he has come to you a couple of times, time might be short. Something must be wrong."

"This is crazy."

"Listen I didn't want to say anything, I thought maybe I was crazy. But I have been noticing things. Fall is coming to early; the leaves are turning; crops seem to be dying fast. Now you have this dream. I think we need to go." Hunter looked into her eyes. Lauren could see the concern there. That he felt something was amiss.

"OK, I'll meet you at my house."

Chapter Seven

Lor floated in and out of memories. Lor was a young man. He was with his dad, trying to talk to him. His father was ignoring him, talking to others around him.

"I have an idea." Lor said to his father. His father kept ignoring him.

"I know how we can fix that." Lor said again.

"Please son, I am talking about things you don't understand."

Lor went to his room and pulled out a diary and wrote in it.

More memories flew by him. They swirled around him making him dizzy at times.

"Make it look like a suicide." Lor said to Curr.

"Don't worry I know what I am doing." Curr said and grabbed the bag of gold from him.

This memory made him cringe. He couldn't believe he had done that, his memories swirled again.

"It's a boy." The midwife said as she came out of the bedroom holding Rex.

"My boy." Lor said with a big smile. Taking Rex from the midwife. That was one of his favorite memories. He loved Rex with all his heart. Memories swirled again. Lor hoped this would stop soon.

"No Ren, I am helping Rex now." Lor had said to his youngest boy.

"But dad I need help." Ren had said.

"Not now." Lor snapped and went back to talking to Rex.

Ren slipped off to his room with his head hanging down.

"Oh my god I acted like my father." The thought ran through Lor. Memories swirled again.

"Why is this happening?" Lor asked knowing he wouldn't get an answer. This time Lor was back at the towers, picking up the sword.

"Why did I do that?" Lor asked himself as he saw himself killing the guard. The guards scream rang in his mind and made him more nauseous than he already was.

The memories swirled again. Lor didn't know how much more of this he could take.

"Son I am going to retire." Lor's father had told him.

"So, I will take your spot?" Lor had assumed.

"No. I am announcing that I am retiring, and Joe is to take my spot."

"Joe? I am the oldest I should be taking your spot."

"You are too self-absorbed. Joe cares about the people."

"I care. I have ideas, but you never listen."

"I'm sorry son, but I have made my decision."

Lor stormed off angry already thinking about how to change this situation.

Lor remembered that angry feeling and didn't like it at all. Lor realized that was when she had started to get to him.

The swirling started again, then slowed and went away. Now bright light surrounded him. He heard voices, familiar voices, but was still unable to answer them.

* * * *

Alastrine rode as the sun beat down upon him, but somehow it didn't feel as warm as it should have. Alastrine looked around and could not believe how fast the leaves were changing.

"Fall is coming to fast." A voice said to him and scared Alastrine out of his thoughts.

"I'm afraid you may be right." Alastrine smiled and said to the farmer who was coming toward him with a cart full of vegetables.

"Had to pull my vegetables early." The man said as he saw Alastrine looking at the cart. "Most of them are still green and will take another week or so to fully ripen."

"Then why did you pull them?"

"Fall is coming quickly. The nights are cold already and the plants are dying fast, so I had no choice."

"I see."

"What does the Goddess say on the matter?"

Alastrine thought for a minute and wasn't sure how he wanted to answer that question.

"Are you OK?" The man asked after a few minutes of Alastrine looking off into the distance.

"Yes, I am fine." Alastrine smiled at the man.

"So, what does the Goddess say?"

"Oh, well."

"You are Alastrine? I mean you have the cloak."

"Yes, I am, The Goddess hasn't said anything about the fall. If it were a problem the Goddess would surely have talked to me about it?"

"Well, that's good to know. I have not been able to get the Goddess to talk to me lately."

"I just talked to her this morning. All is well I assure you." He lied to the man and hated himself for doing so. He thought it better to keep people in the dark, scaring them would only help any shadows that might be around, and he didn't want to do that.

"So where are you off to, need any supplies that I may be able to help you with?"

"I'm." He started to tell the truth then changed his mind. That would only lead to more questions. "I'm off to Lorn to visit the Governor." He lied again.

"Must be staying a while with all those supplies."

"Yes, well I must be on my way. May the Goddess bless you." He said with a wave and rode on.

"May the Goddess bless you as well." The man returned the blessing.

He rode on thinking about his interaction with the man. The plants dying so early bothered him. Something was wrong, and he really needed to get to the elf king as soon as he could. Something else bothered him to. Lying to the man came to easy. He never liked lying, it always made him feel bad, put a knot in his stomach, but not this time. This time it almost felt good, like he enjoyed it. There is only one reason for that, she has somehow tipped the balance. The races have not done anything to tip the balance, but she has managed to tip it anyway.

"I need to get to the elf king fast." He said out loud as he spurred his horse on.

Chapter Eight

George, the son of Barney and Bell, walked by the piers in Moray inspecting the work being done on the boats. He was a big burly man with black hair, beard and brown eyes. He had no time for politics and did not follow his dad's footsteps in the running of Perth. He loved working with his hands, so when asked by his Aunt Sara to come help build boats for the trade route, he was all in. He had been lost for a while after his wife died during childbirth. Barney and Bell had helped him raise his daughter. He knew he would be working a lot of hours when he came to Moray, so he left his daughter with his parents and visited as often as he could. Now she was grown, and he was very proud of her.

"What do you think sir?" A man asked as he was checking the boats.

"These reinforcements on the bow are just what I was looking for." George smiled at him. "This should hold up to the rough waters of Lorn." George patted him on the shoulders.

George had done a great job with the boats. One of the last things Sara did before leaving office had put him in charge of all the shipping routes. That included boat building and maintenance. He loved his job, now a new route with Lorn was coming, and he was going to be ready.

"Oh, George there you are." Came a voice from behind him. He looked back to see Charles coming toward him.

Charles was the head of the city council and had become good friends with George. He was tall and slender. His dark hair framed his narrow face, and his brown eyes always seemed to smile at you.

"What is it I can do for you?" George could tell by his walk that something was wrong.

"It's your cousin."

"Mary Jean? What did she do?" George half smiled. Mary Jean had a habit of frustrating the council because she just could not make a decision.

"I can't find her, and she has not signed the trade route deal yet." Charles was clearly not happy.

"What are you talking about? I talked to her the other day, and she was excited about this deal."

"Well, we passed it two days ago. I went by her office today and she is not there, and the bill is on her desk unsigned. Listen George this should have been done already."

"I know."

"The Governor of Lorn and a representative from the dwarfs are going to be here next week to make it all official."

"I know."

"This city loved Sara; we love Mary Jean to but she."

"I know." George said again a little louder this time.

"One more thing."

"What?" George was clearly annoyed as he turned back to look at Charles.

"There are rumors that Oliver has been advising her again. He is bad news, and the council is very concerned."

"Really." George was clearly angry now. "I will take care of that."

"I hope you can. The council doesn't want to take drastic measures, but it will." Charles said and George looked at him and Charles knew he had said enough.

George turned and walked away muttering to himself about getting his hands on Oliver.

* * * * *

Nasir entered the Garden where the King was talking with Ryo and Felix.

"Your Majesty, you have visitors."

"Please tell them to call back later. I have issues I am tending to right now."

"Your Majesty, It's Luvon and Elyon."

Ayre looked at him surprised.

"They have concerns about the Goddess."

"Show them right in."

"They are going to all show up." Felix said as Nasir left.

Luvon and Elyon walked into the garden and bowed, and the king returned in kind, he had told them a long time ago, they need not bow to him.

"What is it I can do for you?" Ayre asked.

"We were wondering if you had talked to Alastrine lately, Your Majesty." Luvon asked.

"No, I have not."

"We both have meditated and tried to commune with the Goddess, but she has not been there, Your Majesty. Has anyone else had these problems?" Elyon asked.

"As a matter of fact, yes." Ayre said.

"Then do we assume you have also noticed the early fall, your majesty." Luvon asked.

"That is exactly what we are talking about now." Ryo said.

"The wheat crop is dying off already, before it can all be harvested." Elyon said.

"Felix, you have been around the longest, any ideas? Ever see this before?" Ayre asked.

"No, I have never seen this before. I believe she is behind this, but I don't understand what has happen with the Goddess."

"Well, whatever it is, it is going to make this winter very long and hard." Elyon said.

"I am going to send soldiers to help the farmers get as much of the crops in as they can. If things are dying that fast, they will need all the help they can get." Ayre said.

"We need to find answers. More will come here for those answers." Felix added.

"With your permission Your Majesty, Luvon and I can start going through the history books in the royal library to see what we can find." Elyon said.

"The more eyes the better. I have already started looking. I will get the order out to the soldiers and come search with you."

"I will see if there is any elf magic that may help save some crops as well." Ryo said.

"Let's be off. We have a lot to do and not a lot of time. May the Goddess bless us wherever she may be." Ayre said

Chapter Nine

A man walked in the shadows of the dark streets of Moray. A shiny object peaked out of his cloak from time to time. Bars were closing and drunks were stumbling by the man, not even noticing him. Time moved slowly has he worked his way down the streets, finally to a small alley that led to his target. A small house that seemed to set alone at the end of the alley.

"My lady be with me." The man muttered as he picked the lock on the door. In a few seconds he was in and quickly closed the door behind him.

He was standing in a small room that served as a kitchen and living room. There was a fireplace, in front of which sat a kitchen table on a big area rug. A door set off to the right, that went to the bedroom. He lit a match, igniting the oil lamp setting on the table, setting it as low as he could.

"Now where would they be." He searched the room for a hiding spot that held the items he was looking for. He searched the bedroom and found nothing and came back into the main room. The sweat was dripping off his forehead now, he was getting nervous, it was taking too long. Then suddenly when he was by the table the silver object under his cloak vibrated. The man stopped and looked around, then looked down.

"Under the floor." He smiled.

The man moved the table and rug as quietly as he could. There was a trap door.

"Bingo." The man pulled the shiny object from his cloak.

"OK, shadows strike, I need your help." The man reveals a sword in the dim light of the oil lamp.

He tried to open the trap door, but as he figured it was sealed with the magic of the Goddess Atla.

"Easy enough." He said as he raised the sword and struck the door. There was a loud pop and the door opened. The man held his breath waiting to see if anyone outside heard anything. There was silence, so he moved the oil lamp to reveal what was under the trap door.

"What? This can't be!" The man was angry. There was nothing there. The items he had come for were gone, but where? He knew Alastrine hadn't taken them.

Then fear ran through him. He was going to have to tell her that he failed. She was not going to be happy. He closed the trap door and left. No need to tidy up, Alastrine would know as soon as he walked in that someone was there. The man slipped back through the shadows, taking his time till he hit the main road, then quickly to his house and the dark room.

"My lady." He said as he lit the black candle. He wanted to just get this over with.

"You have return quickly. I am pleased." The Goddess Hel's voice was soft.

"Thank you, my lady." The man said wishing he had good news for her.

"Where are the items I asked for?"

"They were not there." The man answered as he held his breath.

"Did you find the hiding spot?" The Goddess's voice was harsh now.

"Yes, Shadows strike had to open it."

"The items were gone?" The Goddess's temper was growing.

"Yes, my lady."

"Her magic is still working. We need to find where the magic sent them." The Goddess told the man who was waiting for her to take things out on him.

"What do you need me to do my lady?"

"Keep working on our other project. I will get back to you when I find out where the items were sent." The Goddess said and she left.

The man breathed a sigh of relief, as he put out the candle and left the room.

* * * *

Arastrude woke confused. She had a strange dream about someone breaking into Alastrine's home. It looked like they were after the magical items but found nothing.

"Where was Alastrine?" She asked as she sat confused on the edge of her bed.

"Mom, are you up?" Came a voice from the kitchen. It was her son. He was there because Arastrude was to leave in a couple of hours.

"Yes, I'm up. I'll be out shortly." Arastrude said as she went to push herself off the bed, and realized there was something in bed with her. She lifted the blankets to see two bows, two swords and four leather bags. Her eyes got big, and she pulled the blankets back over not sure what to do.

"The others are here waiting for you." Her sons voice came again.

"OK, I'll be there in a minute." Arastrude answered.

Arastrude pulled the blanket back again. She took a deep breath grabbed a bag and packed the items with what she needed to take along.

"About time." Arastrude's son said as she came out.

"Sorry, I had a bad night last night." She smiled at him. She looked around and there were two other men there.

"These are the two that are going to go with you to see the elf king." Her son said.

"Hi I am Rulir." The one Dwarf stepped forward without stretched hand. He was a little taller than Arastrude, with short black hair, brown eyes. "This is Dirion." Rulir pointed to the other Dwarf. Dirion was as tall as Rulir, with red hair, green eyes. They were both well built from being in the military.

"We are ready to go whenever you are." Rulir said.

"I will be ready in a few minutes. If you want to wait outside, I will be right out."

"No problem." Rulir turned and Dirion followed him out the door.

"What's wrong mom." Her son asked as the door closed.

"Please be prepared for the worst." Arastrude said and then paused.

"What is it mom?" He asked not sure what she was thinking about.

"I think things are worse than we know right now." Arastrude wasn't sure if she should tell him about what was in the bag.

"OK mom." He looked at her confused.

"I will see you again." Arastrude said.

"Mom, are you OK?" He asked.

"Yes. I just have a lot on my mind." Arastrude smiled and hugged him. She grabbed her bag and headed for the door.

"That's a big bag."

"It's a big trip." She lied, deciding it's best to keep the items a secret.

Chapter Ten

Edo woke, on the fourth morning he was there, shook up. He had dreams again, but this time it wasn't Lor who came to him. It was Rex, at least that's who he thought it was. He had never met Rex, but by how people described him, he was pretty sure that's who had come to him. Rex had asked him to help Lor. He said "Help my dad." Over and over again.

A knock came at his door.

"Yes." Edo answered.

"It's almost noon. Are you ok?" Alex asked.

"Yes, I'm fine I'll be along shortly." He answered shocked at how late it was.

"Listen it's ok. I have a couple of friends coming here for lunch. I'd like you to be here as well."

"Ok, sounds good."

Edo got dressed and noticed the diary was on his nightstand. He picked it up and looked at it. He had not gotten it out of the draw and was confused on how it got there.

"What it is you are trying to tell me?" He asked as he held the diary.

Edo laid the diary back down on the nightstand and sighed heavily. He wasn't getting any answers and wasn't sure where to go to get the answers he needed. He turned feeling a heavy weight on him and left his room. Edo entered the main room where Alex was already talking to his two friends.

"Edo, these are my friends, remember I told you their stand is next to mine. Their children are running it because they had meetings with my father and the council."

Alex's dad, Lor's brother, was still on council. Although now the head of council was elected and not held by a family.

"Yes, of course." Edo smiled.

"This is Tanner and Laura; they have news to share with us."

Tanner and Laura shook his hand, but he saw in their faces the shock of how much he looked like Lor. He knew this was the protector and wielder who had fought against his grandfather.

"I know, not to worry I'm not like him." Edo said with a weak smile.

"Yes, of course." Laura half smiled. "It's just unbelievable how much you look like him." Laura paused. "It's a pleasure to meet you."

Edo had gotten use to the looks over the past several days, many commented on it and he tried to laugh it off.

"It is very nice to meet you." Tanner shook his hand.

"Nice to meet the two of you. I have been told a lot about you." Edo faked a smile. It was nice to meet them, but he had so much on his mind. He wasn't as into it as he usually would have been.

"Well, why don't we all have a seat." Alex offered to break the tension. "I have some fruits, dried meats, cheese and ail." Alex pointed to the small table.

"Thank you." Laura said as they all sat down.

"Well, you know we met with council. We talked about how fall is coming fast and how the crops are dying off." Tanner said.

"Yes, and things seem to be getting worse." Alex said.

"Well, the council agrees. They think we should go see the elf king, to see if he has any idea of what is going on." Laura told them.

"Sounds like a good idea." Alex nodded.

"That's why we are here." Tanner smiled.

"Now I'm confused." Alex looked back and forth at them.

"We need you to help our grandchildren run the stand." Tanner asked.

"Our children have business back in the city they have to tend to. The grandchildren will stay but they are going to need help." Laura explained.

"I'm sure we could do that. What do you think Edo?"

They all looked at Edo.

"Um, what? Sorry my mind isn't here right now."

"Will you help me help them?"

"What do you remember about Rex?" Edo asked to the shock of all of them.

"Rex?" Laura asked shocked at the question.

"Yes." Edo answered his eyes looking desperate.

"Well, He changed a lot during the time he spent with us. He became a very caring man I was proud to call a friend." Tanner said.

"Why the odd question?" Alex asked.

"Can I talk to you guys in confidence?" Edo asked.

"Yes." They all answered.

"I have been having dreams. I wake up sweating and I don't know what to make of them."

They all perked up now.

"With the weird things going on maybe these dreams could have some answers." Laura offered.

"I don't think so." Edo shook his head.

"Well tell us about them." Tanner asked.

"When I was home several nights in a row Lor came to me. He would ask me to help him. We can save them."

They all looked at each other in shock.

"Is there more?" Alex asked.

"When you asked me to come here, I jumped on it hoping the dreams wouldn't follow me."

"And?" Laura asked.

"I was fine till this morning."

"Lor came to you again?" Alex asked.

"No, Rex did. He told me to help his dad."

They all sat quiet for a few minutes.

"I feel like I am going crazy."

"Well, there has to be a reason for this." Tanner assured him.

"We can assume Lor is with the Goddess. He asked forgiveness just before he died." Laura offered.

"There is one more thing." Edo said and got up and went to his room. They all sat looking confused. Edo returned with the diary in hand and laid it on the table. "The morning I left to come here this was on my nightstand. I have no idea where it came from." Edo said.

"What is it?" Laura asked.

"Lor's diary."

They all looked at each other in shock.

"I knew there was one. No one knew what happen to it though." Alex said.

"I know you could use his help here, but I think he should go with us to see the elk king. There is something going on and we need answers." Tanner said.

"One thing we have not told you Alex it that the Goddess has not been answering us." Laura added.

Alex and Edo both looked shocked.

"I will handle things here." Alex said.

"Then we leave in an hour. Bring the diary." Tanner got up and everyone else followed.

"Thank you." Edo said to them as they were leaving.

"You're welcome. We will meet down by the docks in an hour. We will find answers. I'm sure we are not the only ones going to see the elf king." Laura said as they left.

* * * *

"Tell me again why we didn't just take a boat down river." Lauren asked as they walked along the base of the Mountains that lead to the pass just outside of Lorn.

"I want to see if the problems I'm seeing are happening everywhere or just local. The more information I have for the elf king the better the answer will be." Hunter told Lauren as he sighed heavily having to explain for what seemed the hundredth time. They had been walking for several hours and so far, the early fall seemed to be hitting everywhere.

"There look." Hunter put his arm up to stop Lauren.

"What, it's a squirrel?" Lauren said not sure why she was looking at it.

"Yes, look at him he doesn't know what to do. The early fall is catching him off guard."

"So, he is confused."

"Yes, animals have an internal clock that tells them when it is time to do things like get ready for winter."

"This is messing with that clock?"

"Yes, so they don't know what to do now."

"So, what will." Lauren was cut off by an explosion in the woods not far from them.

"What was that?" Hunter asked.

"Look, smoke." Lauren pointed and they both headed in that direction. It didn't take long before they came upon what had made the noise and smoke. There was a tall, slender old lady standing by a cauldron, that sat in front of a small shack. She had shoulder length stringy brown hair, that was turning grey, and brown eyes. She wore a black dress that stopped a couple of inches below her knees with black shoes that covered her ankles. Her long skinny arms were now waving the smoke away from the cauldron.

"I must have mixed those herbs wrong." The lady said as they approached her.

"Are you ok miss?" Hunter asked as they approached.

"Regina." The lady said as she continued to wave the smoke away.

"What?" Hunter asked.

"You said miss. It's Regina. Miss Regina." She was now looking in the cauldron as she spoke to them.

"We heard the explosion and." Lauren started to say.

"Oh yes, well I lost my book and mixed the herbs wrong again." Regina was now looking at several bottle she had on a small table. "Which one did I put in first? Maybe this one." She said holding one bottled up high, so the sun shone through it.

"Are you ok?" Lauren asked.

"You know it's hell when your eyes start to go." Regina said and looked back at them. She gave them a strange look and they both felt weird.

"I'm sorry, who are you?" Regina asked.

"I'm Lauren and this is Hunter. We were" Lauren started, and Hunter cut her off.

"Going for a walk and heard the explosion." Hunter finished and Lauren wondered why Hunter didn't want to tell her the truth.

"Yes, I see. Hunter is it, put some of those logs over there on the fire. Can't have it going out now can we." Regina pointed to a stack of chopped wood. Hunter stood and looked at her.

"Well don't just stand there." Regina pointed again with her long skinny arm at the wood, and Lauren nudged Hunter to go. Hunter sighed and started to put wood on the fire.

"Now what did I do with that book?" Regina said as she looked around.

Lauren looked as saw a book on a stump and went and picked it up.

"You are looking for this?" Lauren asked.

"No wonder I couldn't find it, you had it." Regina said as she took if from her.

"No, it was." Lauren started.

"I don't care if you borrow my book, just ask first." Regina said as she started flipping pages.

"I didn't." Lauren started to say.

"So, you came for dinner?" Regina said and actually looked at Lauren this time.

"What?" Lauren was confused and looked at Hunter who was just as confused.

"Oh, that's enough wood, can't have the fire to hot." Regina said waving at Hunter to stop. She picked up another bottle off the table and held it up to look at the label.

"We didn't" Lauren started again.

"Damned eyesight can't read anything anymore." Regina said as she sat the bottle back down.

"Maybe we should be going." Hunter said looking at Lauren.

Regina looked at Hunter then back at Lauren.

"What is wrong with him?" Regina asked Lauren who looked at Hunter not knowing what to say.

"I don't" Was all Lauren got out.

"Put wood on the fire boy. It's going to go out. Can't finish the spell with no fire now can we." Regina was waving at the stack of wood again.

"Listen we just." Lauren started again as Hunter went back to the wood pile.

"Yes, I know, just wanted to borrow my book. Everyone wants to, but I need it. The memory isn't what it used to be you know."

"No, that's" Lauren started.

"Listen since you are here for dinner the least you can do is help. The stew is in the pot over the fireplace and the bread needs cut it's on the table. I think it is anyway. It's in the kitchen somewhere. Go set the table so we can eat then do this spell."

"We didn't come." Lauren started.

Regina just looked at Lauren and Lauren just started walking toward the shack.

"Now where did I put that book." Regina said as Lauren got to the shack.

Lauren entered the shack, and it was much nicer than she had expected it to be. There was a pot of stew on the fire and a small loaf of bread by the sink. She found some bowls in a small cupboard and dished out some stew in each.

"That's too much wood. I thought I told you to stop." Lauren herd Regina saying to Hunter.

"Dinner is ready." Lauren yelled down to them. The two walked to the shack and as they sat, Hunter rolled his eyes at Lauren who just smiled back at him. They thanked the Goddess for the food and ate quietly.

"Well, you make one heck of a stew, little girl." Regina said as she finished.

Lauren thought to correct her but figured what was the point.

"Thank you." Lauren said.

Lauren cleaned up the bowls and soon joined them outside where Hunter was putting more wood on the fire. Regina was holding three bottles in her hands.

"OK that's enough wood." Regina said to Hunter "Now stand back and hope I do this right." They both backed up as Regina took a pinch out of the first bottle muttered something, they didn't understand, threw the herb in the cauldron. Then did the same with the next two. On the third one they all held their breath. They all breathed out heavily when there was no explosion.

"See I eventually get it right." Regina winked at them.

Regina looked down into the cauldron. "Come come." Regina motioned with her long arms for them to look as well. They both moved slowly and looked into the cauldron.

"The elf king you are going to see." Regina said not looking at them.

They were both surprised that she knew that.

"Many others as well are going. You play a big part in making things right." Regina continued.

"What are you talking about?" Lauren asked.

Regina looked at her and smiled.

"Of course." Regina said.

"Of course, what?" Hunter asked.

"I knew you looked familiar." Regina said as she walked around Lauren.

"What are you talking about?" Lauren asked.

"You are Barney's granddaughter, are you not."

"Yes."

"I was a little girl when the war ended. My family came back to Perth with Barney to rebuild. He was so good looking. I had such a crush on him. You look just like him you know."

"Um thank you." Lauren didn't know what else to say.

"You must go. The Goddess has plans for you two. Must get to the elf king now." Regina motioned for them to go.

"Thank you for dinner." Hunter said as he got to Lauren's side and took her by the hand to leave.

"Oh, where did I put that book?" Regina said as they walked away. "You didn't borrow my book, again, did you?" Regina yelled after them.

"What an odd woman." Hunter laughed.

"Never mind I found it." Regina yelled again.

"Very odd." Lauren added.

"I think we need to get to the elf king as fast as we can." Hunter said as they broke through the tree line at the base of the mountain and heard another explosion.

Chapter Eleven

The morning was cool. Lynn, Dagrel and O put out their little fire as they got ready to go. Dagrel sat on a small rock trying to soak up the last of the warmth from the dying fire.

"What are you thinking about?" Lynn sat beside him.

"It's really cool for this time of year."

"Yes, I agree. Something is wrong. That is why we need to get to the elf king."

"I don't know." Dagrel was looking at the fire and not at Lynn.

"What don't you know?"

"I don't know if that is where we should be going."

"Where do you think we should go?"

"O's dream was about Alastrine needing help. Alastrine is in Moray."

"You assume he is there."

"You assume he isn't."

"I saw you in the cauldron for a reason."

"But what reason?"

"To set you on the right track."

"Are you sure about that?"

"What do you think the reason was then?" Lynn was getting a little annoyed at Dagrel questioning her magic.

"I just think maybe we need to take a step back and ask a question or two."

"Just what question would you ask?"

"If the Goddess hasn't answered anyone. Then who showed you the images in the cauldron?"

Lynn thought for a minute, she found that to be a legitimate question.

"Well, the herbs I used were already bless by the Goddess's magic. So, they would have shown me those things."

"You said that the shadows came through at the end. How much of the vision did they control?"

"The room and everything are protected by the Goddess. Katie's grandparents had put that spell in place."

"Then how did the shadows get in?"

Lynn didn't have an answer for that. She just sat and looked at him.

"I believe in my magic. I believe the things I was shown, I was shown for a reason. The Shadows broke through at the end, that I don't have an answer for."

"O never said anything about the elf king in his dreams. It was that Alastrine needed help." He sighed. "I think we need to go to Moray first."

"That is a long trip, if you are wrong."

"So is the elf king, if you are wrong."

"It is more likely that everyone will end up going to the elf king."

"What if Alastrine is in trouble now and can't get there?"

They both just glared at each other now.

"O not know where Alastrine is." O said as he looked at the two of them.

"You know you are stubborn. Typical Dwarf always has to be right." Lynn said not listening to O.

"Me, What about you. You always rely on magic. I don't trust magic; it has caused more harm to the four races than anything else ever has." Dagrel shot back.

"Well, you didn't have a problem using the magic sword, did you?" Lynn snapped.

"I didn't have a choice." Dagrel was angry that she would say such a thing.

"Please no fight." O said

"I can't believe I even thought to help you." Lynn turned to pick up her pack.

"Fighting bad." O said

"I can't believe we followed you. We lost so much time." Dagrel yelled now.

"Fighting bad." O yelled and then took a step back. They both looked at him.

"What?" Lynn asked him.

"Fighting bad. Help shadows." O said. They both looked at each other in shock that O was the one who had to point that out.

"Thank you, O. You are right." Lynn said.

"So, you can admit when you are wrong." Dagrel said smiling.

"Really, that's what your thick head is taking away from this?"

"That's not all, but it's the first thing."

"O not know where friend Alastrine is."

"How about maybe we escalated into a fight for no reason."

"Yes, that to."

"Friend Alastrine by big house." O said softly

"You are unbelievable." Lynn shook her head, not hearing what O said.

"What big house?" Dagrel looked confused.

"O not know."

"Alastrine lives in a small house in Moray." Lynn said catching up with the conversation.

"No, this big place. Pretty flower and glass."

"How big?" Lynn asked.

"Lots of dwarfs could fit."

"The palace." Lynn looked at Dagrel.

"I think you are right. We need to get moving." Dagrel unhappily admitted.

"Now look who can admit they are wrong." Lynn smiled putting her pack on her back and leading the way.

"That would have been good information to know from the beginning." Dagrel said to O as he started to walk.

"You not ask O." O said as Dagrel walked away from him.

* * * * *

The next morning a cold breeze blew through Moray, as George walked the streets leading to his cousin Mary Jeans house. She was just leaving her house as he was walking up to it.

"Mary Jean wait." He yelled as she walked away from him.

She turned and saw him standing there, he could see she had been crying.

"What's wrong?" He asked as he got to her.

"I made a mess of things."

"It can't be that bad." He said as he gave her one of his bear hugs.

"Two council members were here this morning." She said as he now handed her a hanky to wipe her tears. Knowing now why she was crying.

"And what did they say?"

"They wanted to know why I hadn't signed the trade deal yet."

"And what did you tell them?"

"I said I was having some research done first."

"Go on." He said not liking where this was going.

"They said all the research was done, why was I holding things up for no good reason."

"Why are you?"

"Because." She stopped not wanting to finish what she was going to say.

"Because?"

"Well, I was told that the city could lose jobs."

"The research shows it will create jobs, and I agree with the research."

"Yes, but." She stopped herself again.

"But?"

"Ok don't get angry at me."

"Go on." George knew what was coming.

"Oliver said he wanted to check on some things first."

"Oliver, really you want to take advice from him?"

"I know what everyone thinks about him. I see a different side to him though."

"I know you always see the good in everyone, but you also know what is right and what is wrong."

"Please George not now. I have had a rough morning and I just need a friend right now." Mary Jean's eyes started to tear up again.

"OK, listen let's go inside, sit down and talk this out with common sense." George said.

"That is a good idea." Came a voice from behind George. He turned to see Oliver right behind him.

"Yes, well I wasn't really talking to you, now, was I?" George said through his teeth.

"Well, as you don't know anything about how politics work, and I do. I think that it would be better If I help Mary Jean with this." Oliver stepped in between George and Mary Jean.

"Again, I wasn't talking to you was I." George said clenching his fists.

"Oliver does know more about politics." Mary Jean said softly.

"See this is what I am talking about." George started to say.

"Listen big guy, why don't I take Mary Jean, and we work this out. You go back to building your little boats, and she will talk to you later." Oliver talked down to George as he walked Mary Jean toward the house.

"I'll come down to the docks later." Mary Jean said as Oliver rushed her into the house.

"That little pompous ass." George turned and punched the oak tree that stood at the edge of Mary Jeans yard. He looked at the door they had disappeared through, turned and walked back toward the docks.

Chapter Twelve

The air got cool as the sun started to set. Alastrine wanted to reach Lorn before dark so he pushed his horse hard. He thought to ride straight through the night, but his horse was tired, and he needed to talk to Paxton. Paxton was the Governor of Lorn. he had been working hard with the Dwarfs to get in on the trade route with them and Moray. Alastrine wanted to congratulate him and get a fresh horse. He would have just gotten the horse and kept going, but Paxton would be hurt if he didn't at least stop by and say hi.

"Alastrine, what are you doing here?" A medium build man, with dark hair, and brown eyes, said as he was riding a horse toward him.

"Paxton, where are you going?" Alastrine was shocked to see him leaving the city at this hour.

"I am on my way to Moray."

"At this hour?"

"I just got word that Mary Jean hasn't signed the trade agreement yet."

"What? Why?"

"She has been taking advice from someone."

"Oliver." Alastrine muttered to himself.

"What?"

"Nothing, go on."

"Well, I'm riding all night so I can be there first thing in the morning. I have to get this fixed before the Dwarfs get wind of this." Paxton shook his head.

"The whole route could shut down."

"If it doesn't get signed the Dwarfs won't trust us anymore."

"I told her it was a good plan before I left."

"I was hoping you were going to be there to help me talk to her."

"I have to see the elf king. There are issues that I need help with."

"The early fall?"

"You are very observant. I have always liked that about you."

"There are things happening that are bothering me. Do you think the balance has tipped?"

"No, I don't think it has, but something has happened."

"What do you know about a man named Oliver?"

"Why?" Alastrine asked kind of already knowing why.

"I think he is the one advising Mary Jean."

"He thinks he knows everything but tends to make bad decisions."

"Why would he try and stop this deal?"

"That's a good question. Ever since he and Paul went on a fishing trip late this spring, he hasn't been the same."

"Really?"

"He was always a little strange, but now even more so."

"What of Paul?"

"He never came back. Oliver said he decided to stay. That he got a small plot of land near the lake and was happy there."

"What did his family say?"

"Nothing really. Oliver said he was going to visit, so I guess they figured if he was happy."

"What do you think?"

"Then, I thought nothing of it. Now, I don't know. I hope the elf king has answers."

"I have to get going I have my work cut out for me."

"As do I. Can I get a fresh horse?"

"Absolutely, just go to the stable and they will help you."

"May the Goddess bless you." Alastrine said as he rode toward Lorn.

"May the Goddess bless you, my friend." Paxton said as he headed toward Moray.

* * * *

Ryo stood at the reflecting pond staring at the flat, still waters.

"Is it speaking to you?" Ayre asked as he approached.

"No, it is not."

"Why do you suppose that is?" Ayre asked as the breeze cut through him and made him shiver.

"The wind has a bad feel to it." Ryo raised an eyebrow as he saw Ayre shiver.

"There is something very wrong."

"Any luck in the history books."

"No, but you know that."

"I have never had the pond not respond to me." Ryo said after a few silent moments.

"What do you make of it all?"

"For the first time I don't have a good answer."

"Then we are in more trouble than I thought."

"She is definitely behind whatever is going on." Ryo said not wanting to mention the Goddess Hel's name.

"The balance is not tipped. That even I can tell."

"That is true. She is up to something else and has somehow gotten the Goddess out of the way."

"So, what do we do?"

"Prepare. Hope those on the other side know what is going on and fix it fast."

"Prepare for what?"

"I don't know."

"How do we prepare for something if we don't know what to prepare for?"

"I don't know."

"Well, that isn't what the others are going to want to hear when they get here." Ayre sighed as the last of the sunlight faded away, leaving them standing in the dark.

Chapter Thirteen

Lor heard voices, and slowly recognized a few of them. It was Rex his, son, and Mir, his father, but the others he didn't know. Lor wasn't sure what they were talking about at first, then realized they were talking about him.

"Do you suppose he saw anything?" Rex asked.

"I hope so, we need all the information we can get." One of the strange voices said.

"He seems to be coming around." Mir said.

"Son, are you there?" Lor said as he came around.

"Yes dad, I'm here." Rex answered.

"The Goddess needs help." Lor said being fully with it now.

"Yes, we know, but we don't know what happen." Mir said.

"She tricked the Goddess, got the Goddess on her side of the lake, and trapped her." Lor started talking fast.

"Slow down." The voice he didn't recognize said, and Lor looked toward him and saw a bright light.

"This is Lofiel. He is an Angel that fights the Shadows." Mir said.

"I need to know exactly what happened." Lofiel said.

"I was at the lake." Lor stopped to think for a minute.

"Take your time and think." Rex said.

"Things went all black." Lor said.

"Yes, we know." Rex said.

"He was there." Lor said remembering the Shadow that had controlled him.

"Yes, he was." Lofiel confirmed knowing who he was talking about.

"He said he is attached to me." Lor was scared now.

"He isn't. He lied to try and get you to come over to their side." Lofiel said.

"He is strong." Lor said still scared.

"He can't get to you here." Lofiel said.

"What happen to the Goddess?" Rex asked.

"She came to the lake and was looking in." Lor started and stopped to think. Things were still foggy and he wasn't sure what happened next.

"It's ok, take your time." Mir said.

"She was looking in the lake. Then she showed up. They had words and the Goddess kept backing up from her. She back to the middle of her side of the lake." Lor continued.

"Then what?" Lofiel asked.

"Then she waved her hand. The Goddess Atla was standing in the middle of The Goddess Hel side of the lake. Shadows surrounded her, trapped her. Then The Goddess Hel waved her hand, and a cage was around The Goddess Atla." Lor was choking up.

"What happened then?" Lofiel pressed.

"She took the Goddess into the dark."

"We have to get the angels together and rescue her." Lofiel said and turned to leave.

"Then he showed up." Lor was scared again.

"He can't get you here." Rex said.

"I'm sorry." Lor said.

"For what?" Mir asked.

"I saw my life. I made a lot of mistakes."

"We all did." Mir said.

"You need to relax right now. You have been through a lot." Rex said.

Lor relaxed some and his thoughts drifted to what he had been shown.

* * * *

Tanner, Lora and Edo had left the island and made it to Juna, and the noon sun beat down on them.

"Do you think the elf king will have answers for me." Edo asked for the hundredth time.

"Well, I hope he has lots of answers, but we won't know till we get there." Tanner's face showed how tired he was of that question.

"Let's get something to eat and keep moving." Lora smiled at Tanner and squeezed his hand. "It's a long trip yet."

They move through the streets to a tavern that Tanner and Lora knew well. After the war, Curr had become the Governor of Juna and opened a tavern. Tanner and Lora had been there many times over the years.

"The food here is good." Tanner said as they got to the door.

Curr had passed away a couple of years earlier, but his son Alvin had taken over the tavern and ran it just the same as his dad.

"Well, it's good to see you two." Alvin said as they walked in.

"Thank you." Lora smiled "I'd like you to meet our friend Edo."

"Nice to meet you." Alvin smiled as he shook his hand. "Now no arguing whatever you want is on me."

"This is why we never come here." Tanner laughed. "We can pay for our bill."

"My father would roll over in his grave. He said you never pay." Alvin showed them to a table.

"Yes, I know." Lora sighed.

"Nancy, they get whatever they want." Alvin said to one of the waitresses.

"Of course, they do." Nancy smiled as she walked over. She was a half dwarf half human who had worked at the tavern for many years and knew who Tanner and Lora were. "It's good to see you guys again. I see you have a friend with you today."

"Yes, this is Edo." Lora said as they all sat down.

"Well, nice to meet you, Edo." Nancy smiled again as she went to get the drinks.

"So, what are you doing slumming it in Juna?" Alvin joked as Nancy brought them drinks.

"We are on our way to see the elf king." Tanner almost whispered.

"That's a long trip. Something must be up." Alvin looked around at all three of them.

"There are some questions we need answered and we hope the elf king can help." Lora answered.

"Well, you are going to the right place for answers."

"We hope so." Edo sighed.

"Well, if there is anything you need before you go just let me know." Alvin said and left the table as Nancy was bringing their food.

Alvin joined them a short time later, and they made small talk.

"Well, I'm not sure why you are going to see the elf king, but I have a few concerns." Alvin finally said.

"Really." Lora raised an eyebrow.

"Yes, well things seem to be moving fast this fall. The crops are dying before we can get them all in." Alvin continued.

"Well, that's funny." Tanner half smiled.

"What?" Alvin looked at Tanner.

"That is what we are going for?" Tanner patted him on the shoulder.

"Then it is worse than I thought. Please don't let me hold you up." They finished their drinks. Alvin got them supplies, more than they asked for, and they headed out.

Chapter Fourteen

The morning was cool as Lynn, Dagrel and O pushed forward, they wanted to see the elf king as soon as possible. Clouds were rolling in, it looked like it was going to rain any minute. Lynn and Dagrel were both in their own thoughts. They were wondering how the conversation that morning ended up with them arguing. It had happened so easy and neither liked that.

"O smell something." O said stopping in front of them.

Neither of them heard him and both ran into him.

"What are you doing O?" Dagrel asked as he barely stopped himself from falling.

"Sorry O I was in my own little world." Lynn said as she bounced off of him.

"O smell something." O repeated as he sniffed the air.

"What are?" Dagrel started to say then felt something race through him. Something he had not felt in a long time, and he froze.

"O, what do you smell?" Lynn asked as she noticed Dagrel acting weird.

Dagrel turned and grabbed Lynn by the arm and went into the wood line close by. O followed looking over his shoulder to see if anything was coming.

"What is going on?" Lynn asked as she yanked her arm free, and O motioned for her to be quiet. Dagrel froze as the magic he felt from seventy years ago surged through him like an old friend.

"Bad Trolls." O said.

Lynn looked at O then to Dagrel.

"Is Dagrel ok?" Lynn asked O.

"Bad troll." O said

The magic grew in Dagrel and he wasn't sure what he should do, he didn't have the sword to direct the magic. He did have a sword at his side, but he wasn't sure if it could handle the magic. Dagrel slowly put his hand on the hilt and could feel it vibrate.

"What is going on?" Lynn said as she saw Dagrel's sword vibrate and glow. Then suddenly it exploded into a million pieces.

"Guess that's not going to work." Dagrel said looking down at the shattered sword.

"What happen?" Lynn's eyes were big as saucers.

"Bad trolls." O pointed and they all looked through the trees to see two trolls and a mountain dog walking out in the open, not caring if anyone seen them or not.

"What are they doing?" Lynn asked.

"Looks like they are looking for something." Dagrel said.

"Bad trolls." O said

"Bad trolls and shadows." Dagrel said and Lynn looked shocked at him.

"How do you know that?"

"The magic of the Goddess is running through me."

"That's what exploded your sword?"

"Yes." Dagrel barely got out before the mountain dog looked straight at them. The trolls pointed and the mountain dog came right at them. The magic in Dagrel screamed threw him now, but he could do nothing with it. O grabbed a tree, ripping it out of the ground he came around and caught the mountain dog in the chest sending him flying.

"The traitor." One of the trolls yelled and they both came at O.

Dagrel looked around helpless. His sword in pieces. Lynn pulled some herbs and threw them at O, muttered some words Dagrel didn't understand. The two trolls stopped and looked around giving O enough time to catch one of them on the head with the tree.

"What did you do?" Dagrel asked.

"Made O invisible for a few moments. It won't last long." Lynn said as the mountain dog came back at O.

"Need help?" A voice came from behind them. They turned to see Arastrude standing there digging in a bag and two other dwarfs rushing forward with battle axes drawn.

"Here use this." Arastrude tossed a sword to Dagrel.

Dagrel caught it and recognized it right away. The magic now burst threw him with a vengeance. Dagrel was on top of the troll that O had knocked to the ground, running his sword into his heart, the familiar scream of the shadow from long ago came, then the shadow slipped into the ground. Lynn stood in shock at how fast Dagrel was moving.

"O look out." Arastrude yelled, as the second troll came after him.

Dagrel turned and was on the trolls back and ran the sword in his back. The troll screamed and there was a high-pitched scream. O used the tree again and sent the mountain dog flying again. Dagrel was around O and on the mountain dog in seconds. There was another loud scream and the shadow slipped into the ground.

Dagrel pulled the sword out of the mountain dog and looked at Arastrude as he held up the sword and the magic receded.

"It's a long story I will explain on the way to the elf king." Arastrude said as everyone was looking at her.

* * * *

"This is not good." Felix flew through the doors of the palace and down the hall to the library where Ayre, Luvon, and Elyon were filtering through the history again, because they didn't know what else to do.

"Ayre, I have bad news." Felix said as he flew up in front of him.

"More?" Ayre asked. Sighing heavily.

"This is very bad." Felix was out of breath.

"What is it." Luvon asked.

"The magic was used."

"What magic?" Ayre asked.

"The Goddess's magic. A protector." Felix said and they all looked at each other.

"Are you sure?" Luvon asked,

"Yes. I can feel when magic is used, and I can tell by the strength that it was the Goddess's magic."

"The balance isn't tipped." Elyon said.

"Alastrine hasn't pick the chosen that I am aware of." Ayre said. "He would have contacted me."

"So, what do you think is going on?" Luvon asked.

"I'm not sure, but this raises more questions than it answers." Felix shook his head.

"Well, I am more confused than ever." Ayre said.

"Your Majesty." Nasir said as he entered the room.

"What is it?" Ayre asked, not sure he wanted to know.

"Scouts have come back from the wood line. There are several trolls on the plateau. They seem to be looking for something."

"It just keeps getting better." Felix said.

"Come, we will head out and see what is going on. Luvon and Elyon, I want you to come. We will see if the magic stirs in you." Ayre said.

They all put the books down on the tables and headed down the hall.

"What do you think is going on?" Felix asked Ayre as they got to the stables.

"I don't know, but things seem to be getting worse. I hope Alastrine gets here soon, and he has some answers." Ayre said as he got on his horse.

Chapter Fifteen

The Goddess Atla sat in the magic cell her sister trapped her in. The Goddess had tried to break it several times and had failed.

"Well, I suppose you think you are smart." The Goddess Hel said as she appeared out of the darkness.

"I am not sure what you are talking about." The Goddess Atla replied.

"You put a spell on those silly items. Your keeper left them protected by your spell and when I sent someone for them, they were gone." The Goddess Hel glared at her.

"You don't say." The Goddess Atla replied.

"I will find them and destroy them." The Goddess Hel hissed at her.

"Don't hiss at me. You don't scare me."

"I will." The Goddess Hel floated around her cell.

"You can't hold me here forever."

"I can do what I want."

"Help will come for me."

"No one knows where you are. You came to the lake alone."

"You don't think they will figure it out?"

"Not in time to save the races."

The Goddess Atla glared at her.

"That's right, the longer I keep you here the more souls that will come to me. As for your silly items it's only a matter of time till I find them." The Goddess Hel sneered.

"My lady." A voice came from behind them, and the Goddess Hel disappeared. To reappear seconds later.

"They were foolish enough to use one of the items." The Goddess Hel laughed. "I am going to go myself and take care of them. Soon this will all be over." The Goddess Hel laughed as she left, and the Goddess Atla sank to the floor.

* * * * *

Alastrine rode into the night. The sky was clear, and the stars were bright as he rode through the pass. His thoughts drifted as he rode. He wondered anew why the Goddess hasn't been answering him, or anyone for that matter. Had her sister done something, if so, what? He was so deep in thought he didn't notice things around him.

"Who's there?" He said feeling like someone was watching him.

Looking around he realized how much the clouds had closed in around him.

"I don't like this." He said and pushed his horse harder. He kept looking over his shoulder. By early morning he was leaving the pass and into the open fields. Once he was in the field he pulled up on his horse, that was in need of a break. He looked back at the pass to see what was following him and nothing appeared.

"I don't like this at all." He turned very tired and started riding again. Soon a farm came into site. He rode up to the house, and a man came out.

"Well stranger it has taken you long enough." The man said.

"I'm sorry. I'm very tired. Could I rest here for a while?" He asked.

"What? Alastrine what are you talking about?" The man asked.

Alastrine took another look through his blurry, tired eyes, to see a tall man with blond hair, green eyes and a farmer's tan.

"Kale, is that you?"

"Yes, Come in my friend." Kale said. He was very well built from years of working on the farm.

Alastrine got off his horse and followed Kale in, then into a small room with a bed.

"Here my friend, get some rest."

A few hours later Alastrine woke to hear Kale and his father Adam. Adam was Will's son. Adam was just under six foot tall with dark brown hair and eyes. He was starting to put some weight on as he didn't work on the farm as much now that he was older. Will didn't go back with James to the farm, outside of Moray, after the war. He had met a girl Susan and they stayed just east of the pass and started a farm. Alastrine had visited often to check on because he had promised James he would.

"Sorry my friend, that I didn't recognize you." Alastrine said as he entered the kitchen.

"We have been expecting you." Adam said.

"Why?"

"Things are bad and getting worse." Adam said.

"Really."

"You know, or you wouldn't be here." Kale said.

"You are on your way to see the elf king I expect." Adam added.

"This family has always been too smart for its own good." Alastrine smiled.

"Yes." Adam smiled at him.

"So, what has the Goddess said to you." Kale asked.

"Well." Alastrine started.

"She isn't answering you either." Adam sighed.

"I'm hoping the elf king has some ideas." Alastrine said.

"I'm ready to go when you are." Kale smiled.

"What?" Alastrine looked confused.

"I'm going with you."

"No, you don't need to go."

"I know that I want to go."

"And I told him he had to." Adam said. "This family has always been there for you, and we will be now."

"Ok fine." Alastrine knew it was pointless to argue with them.

"Good, now eat and then you guys can be on your way." Adam said as he put a plate on the table for Alastrine.

Alastrine sat down and ate and soon him and Kale were off.

"Why are we going this way?" Kale asked Alastrine as they headed to the south side of the lake.

"I'm not sure, I just feel this is the way we need to go."

Chapter Sixteen

Tanner, Lora and Edo flew as the sun was heading west for the night. The plateau that had seemed too small at first was now very large and in front of them. The afternoon had been cooler than usual, but the sun stayed out, now clouds seemed to be rolling in as night was approaching.

"I think we may get some rain." Edo said as they flew.

"Maybe we should find somewhere for the night." Lora said.

"I really don't want to get caught in the rain on the open Plateau." Edo added.

Tanner sighed heavy not really wanting to waste time. Especially since Alvin had pulled him aside as they were leaving and warned him that trolls had been seen in the area.

"Really let's land and find some shelter maybe the storm won't last long." Lora offered.

Tanner sighed again and started toward a group of trees that led to the Mountain pass.

"Here comes the rain already." Edo said as they landed.

"That storm moved in fast." Lora said as she darted under some trees.

"It happens." Tanner said downplaying how fast the storm seemed to move in.

"What's this?" Edo asked. he was at the entrance of the mountain pass.

"What's what?" Lora asked as she walked over followed by Tanner.

They both looked down at what Edo was pointing at. Lora looked at Tanner mouth wide open.

"What?" Edo asked.

"That's a troll footprint." Lora said.

"A what?" Edo almost yelled then caught himself.

"A troll footprint, but why is there a troll here?" Lora asked.

"Alvin pulled me aside before we left and said he had heard trolls were out and about." Tanner said looking at the footprint.

"And you didn't tell us?" Lora asked looking at him.

"Because Alvin didn't see any himself. He was going off hearsay." Tanner sighed.

"What do we do now?" Edo asked clearly shaken by this turn of events.

"We need to follow and see where it went." Lora put her hand on her hips.

"Follow?" Edo looked shocked.

"If it went to the temple that could be a problem." Lora warned.

"It? Most likely they." Tanner added.

"You mean there is more than one?" Edo almost yelled.

"I would think so."

"We need to find out and get help." Lora said.

"Let's follow the footsteps and see where they go." Tanner started to walk.

"I can't believe what I am hearing." Edo said.

"Listen she is up to no good and using the trolls again. We need to see what they are up to so we can tell the elf king." Tanner said.

"Tanner is right." Lora added.

Edo sighed. "Let's go." He turned and started walking in the direction the troll was headed as the rain became steady.

After a while of walking Lora yelled through the rain as it started to slow down.

"Over here more footprints. There are several trolls and a mountain dog I believe." Lora said.

"They seemed to have stopped here. There are the remains of a fire." Tanner pointed.

"So, they were through at least a day ago." Edo said as he looked around to see where the tracks led.

"I would think so. There are bones here from whatever they ate." Lora said.

"The tracks go off this way." Edo pointed as Tanner and Lora continued to look around the fire.

"That leads to the plateau." Tanner said.

"That's going to be a slippery uphill walk." Lora looked at the water was running down the stones.

"Let's camp here for the nigh. We know they aren't heading toward the temple, and an elf guard will see them on the plateau." Tanner said.

"Good idea, maybe the morning will not be as wet." Edo said as they all looked for some shelter. They found some big boulders that covered as small indent in the side of the mountain. They crawled inside and took turns on watch.

* * * * *

Mary Jean had her morning coffee and walked out of her house into a damp and dreary day.

"There you are my dear." Paxton said as he came up behind her, scaring her.

"Paxton, what are you doing here already?" Mary Jean asked confused to see him.

"There was rumor that you didn't sign the trade deal, and that you may have some questions about it." Paxton said trying to be as nice as he could.

"No, I'm fine. It's just." Mary Jean stopped not sure what she wanted to tell him.

"Well then let's go sign it."

"Actually, I was on my way to the council hall now. There is a message from the dwarfs."

"Really?" Paxton asked confused.

"Yes, the council sent a message to me this morning."

"May I come with you?"

"Yes." Mary Jean smiled, and they walked to the council hall where the council was waiting.

"Well, Paxton nice to see you." One of the members said as Paxton and Mary Jean entered the hall.

"The news isn't good from the Dwarfs." Another member said cutting off the pleasantry.

"What is it?" Mary Jean asked confused.

"They want to push off signing the deal till after Samhain." Charles said.

"What? Why?" Paxton asked frustration showing in his voice.

"They are concerned that there are other things that need attention right now." Charles said.

"Maybe that is why Alastrine went to see the elf king." Mary Jean said.

"He what?" Charles asked.

"Yes, he left the other day." Mary Jean said.

"Yes, I saw him. It's about the early fall and the crops dying fast. The dwarfs probably are having the same issues." Paxton said.

"It seems you have time on your side now Mary Jean." Charles said and sighed.

"Yes, but the problems the dwarfs and Alastrine are talking about need attention." Paxton said.

"I agree." Mary Jean said.

"This could make for a ruff winter if the food supply is low." Paxton said.

"We need to work together to make sure we will make it through the winter." Charles said to Paxton.

"Can you get word to Perth so Trent can join in." Paxton asked.

"Yes, I will get right on that." Charles said.

"Mary Jean come with me; we will start looking at what needs to be done."

"Ok." Mary Jean said as her head was spinning from everything that was going on.

Paxton and Mary Jean headed toward her house.

"Where are you going?" Oliver asked as he approached them.

"HI, Oliver. This is Paxton, he is the Governor of Lorn." Mary Jean said, Paxton smile faded as he realized who this was.

"Nice to meet you." Paxton reached out and shook his hand and didn't like what he felt from Oliver.

"Yes, nice to meet you. Mary Jean perhaps you and I should go have a talk first." Oliver said as he brushed Paxton off.

"I'm sorry, Oliver is it. We have business to attend to that we don't need your help with, so you will have to talk to Mary Jean later." Paxton pushed by him and took Mary Jean by the hand. Then something fell from Oliver's cloak, and they all looked down.

"Where did you get that?" Paxton's eyes were wide. Mary Jeans mouth dropped as even she recognized it.

"It was a gift." Oliver quickly picked it up.

"That's the sword that." Was all Mary Jean got out before getting cut off by Oliver.

"You two need to come with me." Oliver said.

"I don't think so." Paxton said as he pushed Mary Jean back and reached for his sword.

Oliver stepped up to Paxton and got in his face.

"I will kill you and her before you have your sword pulled. Then I will start with the children of this city." The shadow that controlled Oliver was now talking and growling at Paxton and he slowly pulled his hand away from his sword.

"What do you want?" Paxton asked scared of the answer.

"Follow me, and don't try anything. If you do it will be the last thing you do." Oliver said and turned and started walking. They followed him to his small house just a short distance from where they were. Paxton had hoped to see someone he could send a signal to, but he saw no one.

"What are you going to do with us?" Mary Jean asked trying to hold tears back.

"Cooperate and you will be fine. Now go into that room." Oliver said as he pointed to a door.

Paxton opened the door and entered followed by Mary Jean and Oliver. The room was dark, and they couldn't see anything.

"Stand over in the corner." Oliver instructed as he lit a black candle that illuminated the room very little.

"What are we doing?" Mary Jean asked.

"Waiting for her." Oliver said and Mary Jean and Paxton's heart sank.

Chapter Seventeen

Lauren and Hunter got to the pass just after night fall. They were both tired from walking and found a safe place to rest by the entrance to the pass. They had a small fire and ate a little then sat quietly looking around.

"Something doesn't feel right." Lauren said as she moved closer to Hunter.

"I was feeling the same way." Hunter said and then suddenly the fire went out like it was blown out. They both looked at each other.

"Did you blow out the fire?" Lauren asked knowing it was a stupid question, and Hunter gave her a stupid look, then they both heard a low growl.

"We need to get to Lorn now." Hunter said as he grabbed his bag. Lauren followed suit.

"Which way do we go?" Lauren asked.

It was pitched dark and cloudy. They had no idea which way the city was. Then they heard a growl again.

"The growl is coming from that direction, so we go this way." Hunter said as he pulled his sword. They walked for a long time. Tripping on rocks and small bushes. They both had cuts and scrapes and could hardly keep their eyes open.

"We should had gotten to Lorn by now." Lauren said.

"I know. We must be in the pass." Hunter said not liking what he was thinking.

"Should we turn around?" Lauren asked and heard another growl behind them.

"Whatever is back there won't let us now." Hunter said, "I think it is pushing us this way."

"What?" Lauren was shocked.

"We need to find a place we can take a stand."

"What do you think is following us?" Lauren asked fear in her voice. Hunter looked her in the eyes, and she could see the fear in his eyes.

"You don't know?"

"Shadows." Lauren whispered.

"That lady said we were important." Hunter said as he pushed Lauren to a large boulder and they both climbed it.

"Goddess bless the water and keep us safe." Lauren said as she opened her water container and stuck her finger in it. She spread the water around the base of the rock and poured the last couple of drops on Hunter's sword.

The growling got louder and seemed to be all around them now. It was so dark they had a hard time just seeing each other. Hunter had his sword ready, but Lauren only had a dagger, but she wasn't going down without a fight. Second slipped by, seeming like days. Sweat dripped off their foreheads into their eyes making the little vision they had worse. Then it seemed like something was clawing at the rock trying to get up to them.

"The blessed water isn't working." Lauren said as fear gripped her tighter.

"We will be ok." Hunter said as he swung his sword in the direction of the noise not knowing if he was hitting anything or not. Then suddenly there was a bright light and the noises fled.

"Well, how about that got it right this time." A familiar voice said as the bright light surrounded them giving them a feeling of peace. It took a few seconds for their eyes to adjust but when they did there stood Regina.

"Traveling at night when shadows are after you is not a good idea." Regina scolded them.

"How did you?" Hunter started to ask shaking his head in disbelief.

"Who cares, thank you." Lauren cut him off.

"No time for questions now. That spell won't hold them off forever. Now where is my pack?" Regina asked.

"On your back." Hunter pointed.

"Yes, of course. Then let's go."

"You are going with us?" Lauren asked.

"Well, it seems I have to, now don't I. Can't have the shadows getting you before you fix this mess." Regina said as she started walking. While Lauren and Hunter just stared at her.

"What are you waiting for?" Regina looked back at them. They both sighed and followed Regina.

* * * * *

"Want to explain how you have this?" Dagrel asked Arastrude as he walked to her holding the sword, he hadn't held in seventy years.

"I wish I could." Arastrude said opening the bag so Dagrel could see the rest of the items.

"How?" Dagrel asked not knowing what else to say.

"What is it?" Lynn asked confused by everything going on.

"I have all of the blessed items." Arastrude said as she closed the bag.

"How?" Dagrel said again still in shock.

"I had a dream that someone broke into Alastrine's house to get them. I woke up in bed with them next to me."

"The Goddess had a protection spell on them." Lynn said.

"So, then someone did break into Alastrine's house?" Dagrel asked.

"I would think so." Lynn said.

"So why did they come to me? Is Alastrine ok?" Arastrude asked.

"I think Alastrine Is on his way to the elves. Why they came to you instead of him. I'm not sure." Lynn said.

"I'm glad they did. We would have been killed." Dagrel said.

"What do you think the trolls were doing?" Arastrude asked.

"Not sure let's talk as we walk." Lynn suggested as O threw the last troll into the lake.

"They were feeling the air. Like they were looking for something." Dagrel said as he put his sword away and started walking. He could feel the magic in the sword next to his leg. It felt good.

"It is odd that the shadows seem to be controlling them again. The balance hasn't been tipped." Lynn said.

"But the Goddess is missing, or at least not responding to anyone." Dagrel said.

"She has to be behind all this." Arastrude added.

"That's a problem we can't fix." Lynn said.

"I hope the elf king has some answers for this." Arastrude said.

It was late when they reached the Temple, and they were shocked how unkept it was. Weeds were growing everywhere. The priest had always kept it very tidy.

"Hello anyone here." Dagrel pulled his sword.

They walked around and finally the door to the temple opened and a priest came out.

"May I help you, my children?" The priest seemed frightened.

"We are friends." Dagrel said confused at the priest demeaner.

The priest pointed behind him to O. Dagrel looked back and O was smiling and waving.

"That is O. He is a good troll." Dagrel said.

"And you were going to take him into the city." Lynn laughed to herself.

Dagrel gave Lynn a look.

"Sorry go on." Lynn said.

"We just need a place to rest for the night." Dagrel said.

"Of course. The temple is always open to travelers that need shelter." The priest motioned for them to follow him. The temple was big, and O had no problem walking in it.

"Please have a seat I will get you something to eat." The priest said and walked away.

They looked around the inside was better kept then the outside was. There seemed to be no one else around.

"There are elf guards watching us." Dagrel said.

"Where?" Lynn asked.

"Don't look." Dagrel said.

"They don't trust O." Arastrude said smiling at O.

"O good troll." O said.

"Yes, O you are." Arastrude assured him.

"Here we are." The priest was back with some fruit and cheese. "Sorry we don't have much. The crops are going bad fast this fall." The priest continued.

"Yes, we are on our way to see the elf king to talk about that." Dagrel said.

"With a troll?" The priest said without thinking.

"O good troll." O said.

"Yes, please forgive me." The priest said.

"May I ask a question?" Lynn asked.

"Please." The priest wanted to change the topic.

"Why is the outside so un kept."

"We clean and weed it every morning and by evening it looks like we did nothing."

"Well, that is something else to add to the weird things going on." Lynn said.

"Things just keep getting better." Dagrel said.

"Why what else is going on?" The priest asked.

"Fall is coming fast. Crops are dying fast everywhere." Lynn said.

"Then you must be off to see the elf king first thing in the morning."

"I hope he has answers." Arastrude said.

"I will show you to some chambers to sleep." The priest looked at O. "You may have to sleep in here, the chambers are small."

O smiled and sat back down, and the priest returned with a blanket and pillow for O. The blanket barely covered his shoulder, but O smiled at the priest who smiled back.

Chapter Eighteen

The morning was damp, and it seemed like it would rain at any minute. George left his small house by the cities edge to head toward the docks.

"Not much work going to get done today." He muttered to himself, as he watched the clouds roll in.

"Oh, great you are here." A familiar voice came from behind him.

George looked behind him to see Trent walking up, as a stable boy was taking his horse.

"What are you doing here?" George turned and gave him a big hug.

"Meeting with Mary Jean and Paxton. There are many problems, be glad you're not in politics." Trent smiled at him.

"Don't worry I keep getting drug into things, being related to Mary Jean the council asked me all the time to talk to her." George groaned.

"Well, I have a new problem to add to the list." Trent sighed heavy.

"What?" George asked not sure if he really wanted to know.

"Trolls have been spotted in the farmlands."

"What? Are they destroying things?" George asked shocked at the news.

"No, the early fall is doing enough of that. They seem to be looking for something, but no one is sure what."

"So where are you off to now?"

"Mary Jean's house. Her and Paxton are supposed to be there waiting for me. Why don't you come with."

"Well, it's going to rain so I may as well go with you." George said as he sighed heavy.

They walked the streets to Mary Jean's house making small talk as they went. People hurried around them wanting to get their work done before the rain set in.

"Charles." Trent said as they got to Mary Jean's house.

"Trent, glad you could come so quick." Charles said as he joined them.

"Wish it were more of a social visit." Trent said.

George knocked and they waited but no one answered. George knocked again and still no answer.

"Maybe they went to city hall." Trent offered.

"No, I just came from there." Charles shook his head.

"Well, I know my cousin and she wouldn't go anywhere right now. She thinks everyone is mad at her and she is afraid to face people."

"Why would they be mad at Mary Jean? She is so sweet." Trent asked.

"She has yet to sign the trade deal." Charles said.

"I thought that was a done deal." Trent looked confused.

"Should have been, but Oliver talked to her." Charles groaned.

George tried the door, and it was open, so they went in. They called out to Mary Jean and Paxton with no answer.

"Look her tea from yesterday morning is still sitting here." Charles pointed.

"How do you know it's from yesterday?" Trent asked.

"There are four cups, three council members had tea with her." Charles said.

"I don't like this at all." George muttered.

"Maybe that Oliver knows where she is." Trent suggested.

"Paxton would not have gone with him willingly." Charles said.

"I don't like this at all." George said again.

"Let's go talk to Oliver." Trent said.

They turned and left the house.

* * * *

Alastrine and Kale rode south around the lake, late in the afternoon Alastrine suddenly stopped.

"What is it?" Kale asked.

"I have a bad feeling." Alastrine said as he got off his horse and walked toward the lake.

"What kind of bad feeling?"

"That kind." Alastrine pointed to a smashed old wood box by the shore.

"That's an old trunk. Probably floated ashore during one of the summer storms. What of it?"

"That's not just any box."

"What do you mean?"

"It's the box."

"The box?" Kale asked confusion on his face.

Alastrine started looking around.

"What are you looking for?" Kale asked after a few minutes.

"That." Alastrine pointed.

"That's just a couple of buzzards flying around."

"Let's see what they are looking at." Alastrine said as he started walking.

It didn't take long for them to find what it was. A man lay decaying from the summer sun.

"What the?" Kale said almost sick from the sight of this poor man.

"The sword is free." Alastrine sighed.

"The sword?" Kale asked and Alastrine just looked at him. "Oh, that box, but the Goddess."

"The Goddess has been missing."

"I'll get the shovel."

"No."

"We have to bury him."

"Look at him Kale. What do you see?"

"I see a body that has been here for a while."

"What don't you see?"

Kale looked and wasn't sure what Alastrine was talking about.

"You don't see bugs eating him, even the buzzards are only flying overhead, fighting their instincts to feast. The evil is still in him from the sword, if we touch him that evil could fill us."

"And the Goddess isn't around to help us if it does."

"Sadly, I know who this man is. We will come back when this is all done and take care of him."

"Who is he?"

"A man from Moray named Paul, and I know who has the sword."

Alastrine sighed heavily, as all kinds of bad thoughts were running through his mind.

"Who?"

"A man named Oliver; I need you to go to Moray to warn the Governor not to trust him."

Kale took one look in Alastrine's eyes and knew that he had to go.

"I will send help as soon as I can. Now go and don't waste any time." Alastrine said as they got back to their horses and headed in different directions.

Chapter Nineteen

The next morning the sun peaked through the clouds as Edo, Tanner and Lora started out. None of them especially Edo really got any sleep. Everything was still wet, so they decided to fly but stay low in hopes of not being spotted first.

"What are we going to do if we find these trolls? We don't even know how many there are." Edo questioned again as they flew.

"We will get help if we need it." Lora said knowing that may not be a possibility.

"I just don't feel good about this." Edo said again.

"We know." Tanner responded.

They reached the top of the trail and landed looking around for the trolls. Their footprints had gone, it was not wet here, and the troll's feet had dried.

"There is nowhere to hide here." Edo said looking around.

"I don't see the trolls. Do you think they went across to the woods?" Lora asked.

"The elves wouldn't like that very much." Tanner said.

"What do we do?" Edo asked.

"Well, we wanted to see the elves anyway. Let's keep going." Tanner said as he started walking across the plateau.

"Why are we not flying?" Edo asked.

"Don't want to freak the elf watchers out. They may fire and asked questions later." Tanners said.

"Especially if the trolls have crossed the wood line." Lora added.

"Walking shows we mean no harm." Tanner continued.

"Ok, good idea. I really don't feel like pulling and arrow out of my ass." Edo agreed not wanting any trouble.

Lora laughed and then something caught her eye.

"Look over there." Lora pointed to her left.

There in the distance were three trolls walking out in the open plateau.

"Well, that's one for each of us." Tanner smiled at Edo.

"What?" Edo said shocked.

"Not to worry." Tanner laughed at Edo. "I'm sure the elves already have alerted the king."

"What are they doing?" Lora asked watching them as they walked toward them. Edo staying behind them.

"It looks like they are feeling the air. Like they are looking for something." Edo said looking a little closer as curiosity took over.

"Yeah, it does kind of look like that, but what are they looking for?" Tanner asked.

"That would be the question that needs answering, well that, and why are you here?" A voice came from behind them.

They turned to see a squad of elf bowmen stand there with bows drawn.

"We are friends." Tanner said putting his hands up. Lora and Edo followed suit.

"First trolls and now you are following them. The king is on his way I am sure he will want to talk to you."

"Good we wanted to talk to him." Tanner replied and sat down, and the other two did the same.

* * * * *

Trent, George and Charles made their way to Oliver's house. It wasn't far from Mary Jean's house. He had just moved there this summer. He said he wanted to be closer to Mary Jean as she was the only family he had.

"You think he knows anything?" Trent asked as George knocked on the door.

"He has been with Mary Jean constantly." Charles said as George knocked again.

The door slowly opened, and Oliver stood there looking half asleep and surprised to see them.

"Have you seen or talked to Mary Jean?" George asked.

"No, I am just getting up myself. Why?"

"Well, she isn't home, and we thought maybe she came to see you." Charles said.

"Like I said I'm just getting up."

George looked passed Oliver at his table. Oliver noticed him looking and closed the door so only his face was showing.

"So, did you need anything else?" Oliver asked.

"No, if you hear from Mary Jean tell her we are looking for her." George said.

"Ok, fine." Oliver said as he slammed the door shut.

George, Charles and Trent turned and walked away.

"He is very weird." Trent said.

"Did you notice the table?" George asked.

"I couldn't see it." Charles said.

"Someone is there. There were several dirty bowls setting on the table." George said.

"Then why lie?" Trent asked.

"That's a good question." Charles said.

"He closed the door more when he realized I was looking. He is hiding something." George said

"Do you think Mary Jean and Paxton are there?" Trent asked.

"If they are it's against their will." George said.

"We need to have guards watch his house." Charles said.

"Then let's get to city hall." Trent said.

"If he harms them." George started to say.

"We don't know anything for sure yet. Don't go off the handle yet." Charles said trying to bring down George knowing his temper.

"I will catch up to you later." George said as he walked away.

"Don't go and do anything stupid." Charles yelled after him.

George didn't respond and Charles and Trent looked at each other.

"You don't think he would do something stupid?" Trent asked.

"I think I need to get guards watching Oliver's house for more than one reason." Charles and Trent moved faster toward city hall.

Chapter Twenty

Ayre and his party broke through the wood line to be greeted by an elf guard.

"Your Majesty, there are three hawk people being held just ahead. They say they need to see you."

"Take me to them now." Ayre ordered.

The guard led Ayre and his party to where the hawk people were waiting.

"Tanner." Ayre said as he got off his horse.

"Your Majesty." Tanner said as Ayre approached. Tanner, Lora and Edo all stood.

"They are friends." Ayre said as he motioned the guards to stand down.

"Luvon, Elyon. It's good to see you." Lora said with a big smile.

"I assume you are here about the Goddess and early fall." Ayre said.

"Among other things." Tanner said.

"Other things. Don't know how much more I can take." Ayre said.

"This is Edo. He is the grandson of Lor." Tanner introduced Edo.

"Pleasure to meet you Your Majesty." Edo said as he bowed.

"Lor's grandson." Ayre said as he eyeballed him. "You look just like him."

"So, I have been told." Edo half smiled.

"So why do I have the honor of meeting you?" Ayre asked him.

Edo explained the dreams and showed him the diary.

"Well, Lor had good intentions when he was young. I knew that without seeing the diary. As for him coming to you, I don't know what to make of that." Ayre said.

Edo sighed heavy and put the diary back in his pack.

"Don't feel defeated. Right now, we have a lot of questions that are going unanswered. We will figure it out." Ayre assured him.

"Did you use the protectors magic." Ryo interrupted talking to Tanner.

"No, how could I? I don't have the bow." Tanner answered confused.

"That magic was used somewhere, somehow." Felix said.

"What does that mean?" Tanner asked.

"We are not sure. It's not good in any case." Ryo said.

"Your Majesty." A guard approached them.

"What is it?" Ayre asked not sure he wanted an answer.

"The trolls are approaching the river now." The guard reported.

"Heading toward the temple." Tanner said without thinking.

"Be my guess." Ayre said.

"There is more." The guard reported.

"This can't be good." Ryo muttered.

"A troll and four dwarfs and a human just came on the plateau from the steps." The Guard reported.

"O." Felix and Elyon said at the same time.

"With Dagrel and Arastrude I would assume." Ayre agreed.

"Well let's go then." Ryo said as they all headed toward the river.

* * * * *

Oliver came back in the dark room where He had quickly tied Mary Jean and Paxton up before answering the door. Oliver lit the black candle again.

"My lady." Oliver said.

"Who was at the door?" The Goddess asked.

"George, Charles and another man looking for Mary Jean."

"This could be trouble."

"What should I do my lady?"

"This is tricky. You can't let them go now. They know too much."

"Should I get rid of them?"

"That could tip the balance."

Mary Jean and Paxton looked on in horror as the Goddess was letting them hear what was being said.

"Whatever you wish my lady."

"Oliver you can't mean that." Mary Jean finally said as tears came to her eyes.

"Quiet." The Goddess Hel screamed at her, and Mary Jean froze in fear.

"Whatever you wish my lady." Oliver said again.

"Take them out. The balance will tip and make things even easier for me." The Goddess Hel said.

"Yes, my lady." Oliver blew out the candle and turned to Mary Jean and Paxton.

"Think about what you are doing." Paxton said.

"I must do what my lady asked of me." Oliver said as he turned to pick up shadow strikes.

Paxton had been playing with the rope that Oliver had tide fast, doing a bad job of it. He had his hands untied and pushed himself out of the way of the sword as it came down and crashed onto the floor.

"Don't fight this." Oliver said as he turned toward Paxton, who had untied his legs and was on his feet before Oliver brought the sword up again.

"You can't do this." Paxton said as he got ready to dodge another attack.

Mary Jean managed to get her hands untied and was working on her legs when Oliver noticed her and turned toward her.

"Where do you think you are going?" Oliver asked.

Paxton charged Oliver and almost caught him off guard, but Oliver stepped aside at the last second and caught Paxton on the back with the hilt of the sword sending him to the ground.

"Stop." Mary Jean said as she got to her feet.

Oliver turned to face her, and his eyes were hollow and empty.

"Oliver, I know you're in there. Please listen to me." Mary Jean pleaded.

"Oliver is not here anymore." Oliver said as he pulled up the sword.

"Yes, you are. Ask the Goddess for help." Mary Jean pleaded.

"I only answer to one Goddess now." Oliver said.

Paxton was stirring now, but Oliver hadn't noticed him as he was talking to Mary Jean.

"You love me. You won't hurt me." Mary Jean said trying to keep his attention.

"There is no room for love." Oliver said.

Paxton was up now and charge Oliver again, who was not ready for it this time. Paxton took him out at the knees and sent him to the floor.

"You will pay for that." Oliver said as he placed his hands under him to push himself up.

Mary Jean grabbed the stone candle holder and smashed his head with it knocking him to the floor again. Blood now started pouring from his head.

"You can't kill me." Oliver muttered.

Paxton grabbed a sword that had been standing by the door.

"May the Goddess bless this sword." Paxton said as he ran it into his back through his heart and into the floor. More blood was pouring out of his body.

"She can't help you here." Oliver placed his hands to try and push himself up again.

Paxton quickly kicked his hands out from under him and his head hit the floor hard. Mary Jean grabbed a dagger off the alter and drove it through his one hand and into the floor so he couldn't move that hand.

"What do we do now?" Mary Jean asked.

"He is possessed by a shadow. Nothing we do will kill him." Paxton said.

Oliver started to stir again, and Paxton took the candle holder and wacked him over the head again.

"I think we need to get out of here. This isn't safe." Mary Jean said as the sight of all the blood was making her sick.

Paxton looked around the room found a couple of short swords and ran one through each of Oliver's calves and into the floor and another dagger which he used in the other hand.

"That should hold him till we get help here. Let's go." Paxton said as he opened the door. Mary Jean followed him out.

Chapter Twenty-One

Alastrine woke the next morning. He had made it around the most southern part of the lake and was now heading north. He wanted to reach the temple as soon as he could, hoping he would be able to talk to the Goddess there.

The morning was brisk as he started out. It would be a long day as he hoped to make it to the temple by night fall. That meant no time to stop, but by mid-morning he had come across tracks that would change his plans.

"Trolls and mountain dogs here." He said out loud to himself. Looking around he found more tracks.

"Looks like several, maybe ten or so. Came through a week ago maybe." He thought for a moment. "I wonder if this has anything to do with the feeling I had. I could swear that the Goddess's magic was used, but how?" He said thinking out loud, as he got back on his horse more confused than ever.

He rode and kept looking for tracks which slowed him down, and he gave up on the idea of reaching the temple by night, but he needed to figure out where the trolls went. Just after lunch he came upon a fishing dock. He stopped and got off his horse and walked around. The trolls had been by there he saw the tracks.

"Anyone around?" He yelled and got no response. He walked around more and went down by the docks and there was a man torn to pieces. He just looked in disbelief.

"They were here several days ago." A female voice came from behind him. He turned and looked around not seeing where it came from.

"Down here." The voice came again. He looked down to see a door of a root cellar barely open and a pair of frightened eyes peering out.

"It's safe you can come out."

"I'm scared. They came out of nowhere."

"They are gone." He reassured her.

"Why are they here?" The lady asked as she still didn't move to come out.

"I don't know."

"Why are you here? Who are you?"

"I'm Alastrine, and I am passing through."

"Alastrine, you are the keeper?" The lady came out of the cellar now, followed by three young children.

"Yes I am." Alastrine said as she hugged him.

"My husband." The lady said as she looked at the dismembered man. Tears came to her eyes.

She was a human, dwarf mix. He wasn't able to tell by looking at the husband because of how bad he had been torn apart. She was short like a dwarf with blond hair, and facial features more on the dwarf side. The children had more human features than she did.

"Pack up the children, come with me to the temple. They will help you there."

"Thank you." The lady said and turned to the children. She had them get what personal things they could carry. There was an old cart that he hooked his horse up to and had everyone climb on board. They were soon on their way. He knew he was doing the right thing but was frustrated because it was slowing him down even more.

* * * *

The night had drug on slowly and Regina, Lauren and Hunter picked their way through the pass. Regina would shout some words every once in a while, to make sure the shadows stayed away. Sometimes she got it right and there was light for a little while, sometimes she got it wrong and there was an explosion and a flash of light.

"Either way they are scared off." Regina had laughed.

They both had laughed it off, but Regina scared both of them. They didn't understand what kind of magic she was using, and worse they were worried Regina didn't know either.

By morning they were out of the pass and exhausted.

"I think we need to take a break and get some sleep." Lauren said.

"I agree, I don't think I can take another step." Regina agreed.

"OK, let's go over by those group of pines. We should get some shade there." Hunter pointed.

"Looks good to me." Lauren said.

"We will take turns watching. I will go first." Hunter offered.

"Watching what?" Lauren asked confused.

"Keep watch. So, nothing surprises us." Hunter explained.

"Oh, I see." Lauren said feeling stupid.

"Well, since you are taking the first shift. We ladies are going to catch some shut eye." Regina said throwing a blanket on the ground.

Lauren joined her and Hunter sat by a tree close to them.

"Can I ask a question?" Lauren asked Regina as they laid there.

"Sure honey."

"How did you catch us in the pass. We left you at your house."

"Honey after you left, I looked back in the pot and saw the trouble you were going to run into. So, I packed up and followed the deer trails over the mountain. It was a straight shot to you."

"I see."

"Remember honey the easiest way isn't always the best way."

Lauren laid back thinking what a great thought from an odd lady.

A few hours later Hunter woke Lauren up.

"We need to get going." Hunter said.

"What huh?" Lauren rubbed her eyes and stretched.

"It's late morning. We really need to get moving." Hunter said.

"You didn't wake me to watch." Lauren said as she ate some dried fruit as they walked.

"You had a long night. It's going to be a long day. Thought you needed the rest." Hunter said smiling at her.

Lauren looked and saw Regina on a horse and two other horses standing there.

"Where did they come from?" Lauren asked confused.

"I have a friend who I do spells for from time to time not too far from here." Regina said. "Didn't even cross my mind till I woke up we could have crashed there." Regina laughed a little.

"Doesn't matter now. At least we have horses." Hunter said as he sighed.

Lauren smiled Thinking what an odd lady she was, and how much help she was at the same time. Lauren got on her horse and they were on their way.

Chapter Twenty-Two

Kale got back to the farm and told his father what had happened. It was already dark, Kale left with a fresh horse in hope of making the pass by morning. Kale had planned on riding all night. He really hated that thought, but he needed to get to Moray before something bad happened.

Kale rode and just before the sun came up Kale came upon another farm. Two Trolls were attacking the farm and the farmers family, who were trying to get the small children to the root cellar. Kale pulled his long sword and charged the trolls.

The farmer saw Kale coming. The farmer had been using his long sword to keep the trolls at bay but was losing ground. Seeing Kale gave him hope and he pushed back against the trolls. The farmer was half human half elf and was very light on his feet, so he was able to move out of the way of the trolls fast. He had cut the trolls in several places and blood was flowing but that didn't slow them down.

Kale rode up behind one of the trolls. The troll heard him just in time and turned to see Kales long sword cut into the troll's right shoulder and across the troll's chest. The impact was so hard it knocked Kale right off his horse.

"Move!" The farmer yelled at Kale, who rolled out of the way just before the foot, of the troll he had attacked, landed where his head was. Kale got to his knees as the troll's club came down and caught him in the ribs sending him flying across the ground. The other trolls were still attacking the farmer, wanting to rip him to pieces, but he was just a little too quick for them. Suddenly arrows were flying into the trolls. Kale looked to see where they were coming from. There were two women on the roof of the house sending arrows as fast as they could. Kale got up as pain ripped through his body like lighting, but Kale pushed through it. The troll that had attacked him now had his attention on the roof of the house as two arrows had hit him. Kale took the opening and ran his long sword into the troll's heart. The troll dropped dead, and a shadow slipped into the ground. The other trolls saw what happened and came after Kale who tried to ready himself, but the pain was getting the better of him.

"I'm coming." The farmer yelled as he ran after the trolls.

The two women sent arrows into the back of the trolls but that didn't slow them down at all. The trolls came at Kale with their clubs raised. Kale held his long sword up. As the trolls got to Kale, he tried to sidestep them, but was way too slow. One of the trolls came down with his club and caught his left shoulder, sending him flying in blinding pain again. Kale pushed through the pain again and picked up his long sword. The farmer was by his side now as the trolls came back to attack again. Suddenly there were arrows again this time one went right into one of the troll's eyes. The troll dropped his club to pull it out, and Kale took the opening and ran the long sword into the heart of the troll. The troll dropped dead, and a shadow slipped into the ground. The last troll had gone after the farmer, who side stepped him catching him in the knee with his sword, which caused him to stumble, trip and fall over some rocks. Kale seeing the opening ran and jumped on his back, as he tried to stand, running his sword into his heart, again sending a shadow screaming and the troll dropped dead. Seeing he was now safe Kale dropped to the ground.

"How did you do that?" The farmer asked as he got to Kales side.

"This sword was blessed by Alastrine and the Goddess many years ago." Kale said and then blacked out from the pain. The farmers wife and daughter who were firing the arrows were soon at Kales side as well. They got him into the house and on a bed to fix his wounds.

* * * *

The Goddess Atla watched as a new shadow was now watching over her. After a few seconds she knew which shadow it was. The Goddess had tried to talk to other shadows, that had been sent to keep an eye on her, but none would respond to her. The Goddess felt sure she could get this one to respond.

"Demoted to guard duty I see." The Goddess said mocking him.

The shadow just turned away from the Goddess and groaned.

"Well failure does have its consequences."

"What are you talking about?" The shadow snapped.

"You are the shadow attached to the sword at the bottom of the lake, are you not?"

"Shows how much you know."

"What don't I know?"

"My sword, shadow strikes, is free, and I will soon be reunited with it."

"But here you are on guard duty."

"The Goddess asked me here, because your angels are attacking her at the lake of souls."

"I see, so you are not strong enough to fight my angels."

"You know nothing."

"I know more than you think."

"Really, what do you know?"

"I know a human has your sword."

"Is that what you think?"

"That's what I know, not to worry he will fail."

"You are here in a cell. Seems you failed." The shadow was smug.

"Oh, I will get free."

"Not before it's too late."

"Too late for what?"

"Too late for you to stop my Goddess from destroying everything you hold dear."

"She has no plan. The balance is fine so she can't release you onto the races."

"Shows how little you know about my Goddess."

"Shows you are too trusting of her."

"Since it doesn't matter anyway, I will tell you what she is going to do."

"Please tell me this fantasy. I would love to hear it." The Goddess mocked him again.

"On Samhain, the vale is at its thinnest."

"Yes, go on."

"It is also a dark moon. She is going to use dark magic to cut the vale for good.

Then we will be free to cross over whenever we want."

"Thank you."

"For what?"

"Your help."

Just then several angels appeared led by Lofiel, who attacked the Shadow guarding her. The other angels attacked the cell she was in. The Goddess sent light blasting the cell into pieces. The Shadow lay on the ground injured badly.

"Did you really think I could be kept prisoner? I waited till I could get the information I needed, and I thank you for that. Now to go tend to my sister."

Lofiel went to finish off the shadow, but the shadow slipped into the ground and got away.

"No matter." The Goddess said. "We have the information we need. Let's go."

Chapter Twenty-Three

"What did we do?" Mary Jean sobbed as she stopped in the kitchen, grabbing a chair to stop herself from collapsing.

"We did what we had to do." Paxton said as he was shaking.

"We killed him. We killed a man." Mary Jean was almost screaming now.

"He wasn't a man anymore." Paxton assured her, trying to hold himself together.

Mary Jean ran to the sink and vomited.

"Didn't you recognize the sword?"

"What?" Mary Jean turned and looked at him.

"The sword was Lor's sword."

"What?" Mary Jean was confused.

"Oliver somehow got the sword out of the lake. The Shadow that is attached to that sword is now in him."

"I don't know." Mary Jean said as she shook her head.

"Oliver is no more; the shadow has control now. He follows her now." Paxton was almost yelling.

"We need to get help." Mary Jean was crying.

"Let's go to city hall." Paxton took her hand.

"He lied to me." Mary Jean said as she was starting to realize what was going on.

"Yes, he did." Paxton said as he helped her to the door.

Mary Jean and Paxton got out of the door and started down an alley.

"I need to sign the trade deal." Mary Jean said after a few minutes.

"Ok we need to get help first." Paxton said.

"I let him trick me. I could have tipped the balance." Mary Jean said after a few more minutes.

"It's ok. He was a friend you thought you could trust." Paxton tried to comfort her.

"There you two are." Came a familiar voice from behind.

Mary Jean and Paxton turned to see George standing there, and his shocked face at seeing the two.

told them how bad they must have looked.

"What happen to you two?"

"Oliver kidnapped us last night." Paxton said.

"I knew it." George said as his face got red.

"We killed him." Mary Jean said tears in her eyes again.

"You what?" George said shock in his voice.

"He has the sword." Paxton said.

"What sword?" George asked.

"He was going to kill us." Mary Jean sobbed.

"Ok I heard enough." George said and turned and headed toward Oliver's house.

"He is dead." Mary Jean said as she followed him.

They made their way back to Oliver's house and the door was open.

"I closed the door when we left." Paxton said.

They went in slowly looking around.

"We left him in that room." Paxton pointed to a door that was open.

"I thought we closed that door." Mary Jean said.

They pushed the door the whole way open, and Oliver was not on the floor where they left him.

* * * *

Kale woke unsure of where he was. He tried to move, and pain shot through every part of him. He laid back and tried to remember what had happen then it all came to him. He tried to sit up again remembering what he was sent to do. He left out a yell this time that brought a lady running into the room.

"Well, you're awake that's a good sign." The lady smiled at him as she offered him some water.

Kale drank slowly and then nodded he had enough.

"You took quite a beating." She smiled at him again and he return the smile.

"I have to go." Kale said and pain shot through him again and stopped him in his tracks.

The Lady pushed back his sandy brown hair that had fallen in his eyes.

"I don't think you are going anywhere just yet." She smiled at him.

"I have to get to Moray. Alastrine sent me there is trouble." Kale spoke through the pain.

"Yes, I know there is trouble. Mike will be in shortly maybe he can help you."

Kale looked at her for the first time. She had long black hair pulled back and brown eyes. Five and a half foot tall and very slender. She wore a light blue dress to her ankles where boots cover her feet.

"I'm sorry, but who is Mike?" Kale asked trying to clear his head.

"That would be the man you save three days ago. My husband." She smiled at him. "I am Ruth, and our daughter is Helen."

"Three days ago!" Kale couldn't believe he had been out that long.

"Yes, we were worried you might never wake up, but here you are." Ruth smiled at him. "We are very grateful that you saved my husband." Ruth used the cool cloth to wipe is forehead.

"I really appreciate all you have done for me, but I must go." Kale started once again.

A knock came at the door, and it opened slightly. A man with brown hair peaked in.

"He is awake." Ruth said to the man as he entered.

"Well thank the Goddess." Mike said.

"This is my husband, Mike."

"What is your name young man." Mike asked. Mike had deep brown eyes and built like and elf, He was still well built from working on the farm. Kale thought he wouldn't want to have to fight him, even if he was a hundred percent.

"I am Kale. Me and my father have a farm not too far from here." Kale smiled not sure how accurate he was about how far he was from home.

"Well. what brings you this way?"

"I was with Alastrine, he has sent me to Moray with a message for the Governor."

"Well, that may have to wait a while, you are hurt badly." Mike talked to him like a father talking to a son.

"Yes, well I don't have that kind of time." Kale said and this time when he went to get up, he managed to sit all the way up.

"I can't stop you If you want to go, but you are in no shape to travel." Mike scolded him.

Kale looked at Mike and laughed to himself. He could stop me very easily if he wanted to. "I appreciate your concern, but I mend fast and will be fine." Kale said as he set his feet on the floor, smiling through the pain.

"Yes, I see that." Mike half smiled. "It's almost night fall, wait till morning and I will have your horse and supplies ready for you."

Kale just looked at Mike for a moment.

"It's not safe to travel at night." Ruth chimed in.

"Ruth has dinner ready. You can join us and get a good night sleep." Mike pressed.

Kale sighed not really wanting to waste any more time, but knew it was a bad idea for him to travel at night.

"Ok, I'll get dress and be right out."

Ruth laid his clothes that she washed and mended beside him on the bed, and her and Mike left the room. It took Kale longer than he thought it would to get dressed. He slowly made his way to the table where Mike, Ruth and who he assumed was Helen sat waiting for him. Two younger children sat at a smaller table to one side of the kitchen.

They ate with some small talk. Kale made his way back to his room where, Helen brought some water to wash up and he went back to sleep. Glad he had chosen to stay.

Chapter Twenty-Four

"You fool you let her get away." The Goddess Hel was Yelling at the Shadow that once use to possess Lor.

"She tricked me my lady." The shadow tried to defend himself.

"Yes, and I am sure you fell right into her trap." The Goddess Hel spat at the shadow as she stormed around the room that once held her sister captive.

"I am sorry my lady." The Shadow offered.

"She still doesn't know what I am planning, so we still have the upper hand." The Goddess Hel said to herself out loud, and the shadow pulled back.

The Goddess spun around to look at the shadow, anger was felt throughout the room. "Your thoughts betray you. You told her didn't you." The Goddess screamed already knowing the answer.

"She was saying how I messed things up last time and putting me down." The shadow started to defend itself again.

"You have failed me for the last time." The Goddess Hel said as lightning bolts roared from her into the shadow leaving nothing but dust in their wake.

The goddess Hel now turned to the shadow that had alerted her to The Goddess Atla's escape.

"You are now the caretaker of the sword. Fix what he had done with the human. Get him out of there and safe till we need him." The Goddess Hel ordered.

"Yes, my lady." The shadow replied and was gone.

"Somehow her angels found out what happen much faster that I had thought. I must have been seen at the lake, but by who." The Goddess Hel muttered to herself. "No matter, my sister will be weak and need time to recover. I have a small window yet." The Goddess Hel said and was gone.

* * * *

Lauren rode slow behind Hunter and Regina. Regina would pull different jars from her bag and always put them back when Hunter shook his head no. Regina would wave her hand, and argue with him but he didn't give in. Lauren ran her hand through her hair and sighed. She was used to washing it every day and it was now dirty, and she hated that.

"He is so stubborn." Regina's voice broke her thoughts. Regina had gotten tired of arguing with Hunter and had ridden up beside Lauren without her realizing it.

"Is he?" Lauren asked.

"All I wanted to do was a couple spells to slow time till we got to the elves, and maybe a weather spell or two so that it stayed nice for the trip." Regina was talking with her hands again now.

"I see. I take it he didn't like that idea." Lauren smiled.

"He said I shouldn't mess with nature. That nothing good can come from that." Regina said as she sighed heavy.

"I think I tend to agree with him." Lauren smiled again.

"Where is your sense of adventure?" Regina asked.

"Look it's a nice day. The sun is warm. Why mess with that?" Lauren asked as she pointed to the sky.

"Because my left hip tells me different."

"Your hip?" Lauren said confused.

"Yes, when the weather is about to change, I get pain in my hip." Regina pointed to her hip.

"You sure it's not just from riding for so long?" Lauren asked.

"Now you sound like him." Regina pointed at hunter who was still in front of them.

Lauren looked at Hunter and smiled. She was glad to have him in her life. She could hear Regina still going on about the weather and was trying to block her out. Lauren was thinking about what she would be doing if she were home.

"Lauren!" Hunter yelled as he charged back toward her and Regina with his sword drawn.

Lauren shook her head and looked around just in time to see a troll coming at her with his club raised. She ducked just in time but lost her balance and fell off her horse knocking the air out of her, her horse got spooked and ran. Hunter came flying by Lauren and struck the troll across the chest and the troll let out a yell.

Lauren rolled to her left and the troll stomped where she had just laid.

"Be gone you nasty thing." Regina yelled as she tried to control her horse.

Lauren scrambled to her feet and turned to run from the troll. The troll took another swing at her, Lauren leaned to avoid getting hit. She tripped over her feet going face first into the dirt. Hunter rode up and leaped from his horse onto the trolls back, driving his sword into the troll's shoulder. The troll twisted and threw Hunter to the ground leaving the sword in his shoulder.

Regina had gotten off her horse and was now pulling herbs from her bag. Throwing them in the air and chanting, explosions suddenly went off around the troll. Hunter took advantage while the troll was distracted. He jumped on the trolls back again, pulled his sword out and shoved it through the troll's heart.

Lauren saw the troll stumble as she was getting to her feet. She ran right at the troll tackling the troll's lower left leg, causing it to fall. As the troll fell Hunter pulled his sword and ran it into the troll's heart again.

They all waited for a second and the troll started to get up again to the surprise of Hunter and Lauren. Regina was there with more herbs sprinkling them over the troll's head and chanting again. In seconds the troll was snoring.

"What did you do?" Hunter asked as he pulled his sword free yet again.

"A sleeping spells." Regina smiled.

"But the troll should be dead?" Lauren was still shocked.

"Not when a shadow possesses it." Regina said.

"Yes well, we need to get moving. This spell may not last long." Hunter said.

"For once I agree with you." Regina said as she got onto her horse.

Hunter looked at Lauren. "Are you OK?"

"Yes, are you?" Lauren smiled back at him, as she brushed dirt off her clothes.

"I think so. You should ride with me till we catch up to your horse." Hunter got on and helped Lauren on behind him. "It looks like your horse stopped there." Hunter pointed a couple hundred yards away.

"You know, I knew something bad was coming. My hip was hurting." Regina said as she rode up. "I tried to tell you."

"You said bad weather was coming." Hunter corrected her.

"No, my shoulder hurts with bad weather. My hip hurts when negative things are about to happen. Honestly do you ever listen." Regina said talking with her hands again.

Chapter Twenty-Five

The woman sat beside Alastrine as he drove the wagon. The children sad in the back with blankets over their heads. They were so quiet you would have never known they were there.

"So, what happen?" Alastrine finally asked.

"It all happens so fast."

Alastrine just looked at her and waited for more.

"It seemed like the troll was looking for something. We didn't know what to do. So, my husband went out to try and get him to leave." The lady stopped for a moment as tears filled her eyes.

"I am sorry." Alastrine said comforting her.

The lady put her hand on Alastrine's leg. "I thank you." She said trying to compose herself. "He went out and asked why you are here?" The lady started again as her big brown eyes were still filled with tears. "The troll acted like he didn't even hear him. So, he yelled, not wanting to get to close, why are you here?"

Alastrine looked over at her. Her head was hung now, and tears came freely.

"You don't have to talk anymore." Alastrine told her.

"It's just so hard, when you don't even know why things happen. I mean my husband didn't even have a sword." The lady sobbed.

"I know." Alastrine replied sorry he even asked her.

"The troll turned, and I could see in his face what was going to happen. I yelled for him to come back into the house." The lady spoke softly.

Alastrine just looked at her. "Would you like some water?" Alastrine finally said offering her his canteen.

"He yelled for me to get the children and hide as he stood his ground." She continued and then noticed Alastrine handing her the canteen. "Thank you very much." She took the canteen and drank and handed it back to Alastrine.

"So, I got the children and all I could hear was his screams as we got into the root cellar. I don't think I will ever forget those screams." She took the old cloth from her sleeve again and blew her nose.

"We are at the bridge now. Once we cross over, we will turn right, and the temple isn't far from there. I wish there was more that I could do for you." Alastrine said to the lady.

"You have helped a lot. I was scared and had no idea what to do. You are a good kind person. Thank you."

"It is getting late. We will make camp on the other side of the bridge. With trolls about they will have the temple locked down for the night before we get there." Alastrine informed the lady.

"Is it safe." The lady asked clearly still scared to death.

"Yes, we will be safe." Alastrine tried to comfort her.

They crossed the bridge and just on the other side they made camp close to the right. Sleep did not come for any of them.

* * * * *

Pain swept through him again and he tried to gage where he was and what had happened.

"He ran swards into my arms and legs. I'm stuck to the floor." Oliver heard himself say. The pain came again, and He wasn't sure how much more he could take. He thought he was moving but how could that be.

"Relax my son." Came a voice. He knew the voice but couldn't remember who it was.

"Help me." Oliver said to the voice not really caring who it was.

"The trolls will help you." The voice came again.

"Did the voice say trolls?" Oliver wasn't sure the pain was rolling through again and he almost didn't care who was helping him as long as he got help.

"They will be looking for you. The trolls will help you stay safe." The voice said.

"Looking for me? I'm here on the floor." Oliver said to the voice.

"No, you are on your way to a hiding place I have picked." The voice came again.

The pain struck like a lightning bolt, and he was out once again.

Oliver's body moved along the wood line outside of the city. A shadow had taken over his body and was taking it toward the mountains. Several people had seen him and quickly walked away. Oliver's eyes were vacant and his skin a pale white. His body was covered in a mix of blood and dirt. Oliver was dragging a sword as he moved. He more floated than walked as his legs never really moved.

"Get him into the woods. They will be looking for him soon." The Goddess Hel told the Shadow.

* * * * *

As the odd group entered the plateau, they could see a cloud of dust way off in the distance.

"Well looks like we attract attention wherever we go." Lynn laughed and looked at O who smiled and shrugged his shoulders.

"It's odd for elf horsemen to be on the plateau." Dirion said looking concerned.

"I agree I would have thought we would have run into bowmen at the wood line." Rulir added.

"Well, this is a strange time." Arastrude said.

"Should we go meet them?" Lynn asked as she started walking.

"Might as well." Dagrel said as the rest of them followed Lynn.

As they got closer to the river, they were shocked at what was on the other side.

"Are those trolls?" Rulir asked shock in his voice.

"Bad trolls." O said.

"What are they doing here?" Dirion asked. "This close to the elves."

"They elves won't stand for this." Dagrel said as he felt the magic in his sword awaken.

Just then arrows came as elf bowmen approached. Two mountain dogs appeared out of nowhere and attacked the bowmen, making short work of two of them. The rest headed for the wood line and trees for safety. They shot many arrows into the mountain dogs with no results.

"They need help." Lynn yelled pulling out her wand and running, followed by Dagrel who already his sword had out as the magic exploded through him again. Rulir and Dirion followed with battle axes drawn. O looked at Arastrude who didn't move.

"Go help them." Arastrude said, as she sat her bag full of the magical items down. O raced to catch the others and in no time was there.

Lynn had gotten close enough and she mumbled some words and directed her want toward the mountain dogs. A north wind came, and the mountain dogs were frozen solid. In moments Dagrel was on top of the first one running his sword into the dog's heart.

Rulir and Dirion looked in time to see half a dozen or more trolls screaming and running toward them. Suddenly elf arrows were overhead again raining down on the trolls but not slowing them down. O tackled the closest troll. More arrows flew and hit their marks, but still not having any affect. Dagrel dispatched the other mountain dog and turned his attention to the trolls. Lynn left loose with another spell, but this time it hit and invisible wall and bounced back at her. A bright light flashed around her and she was gone, and her wand dropped to the ground bouncing around.

Everyone stopped for a moment in shock and then continued fighting. Dagrel had taken out a troll and jumped on the back of another. Arastrude sat on the ground with her palms flat on the ground and started to meditate.

As the trolls started to push back tree roots wrapped around the feet of the remaining trolls and worked their way up and engulfed the trolls in seconds. There was a scream, and the shadows left the trolls and where the trolls had been now stood four oak trees full of leaves.

Everyone looked around for a moment, then all looked over to see Arastrude pulling her hands off the ground.

Chapter Twenty-Six

"MJ is calm for now and resting." Paxton said as he handed some papers to Trent. "She signed the trade agreement, but she wants to leave with me in the morning. She is scared Oliver is going to come after her." Paxton said as he took a seat in MJ's living room.

"Can you blame her?" Trent asked.

"I will take this to the council tomorrow." Charles said, "We will elect a temporary Governor until she can resume her duties."

"She has been through a lot." Paxton shook his head. "I can't believe what happen, she was so close to Oliver."

"We need to find Oliver." George chimed in.

"We will get a search party together asap, but he can't be far as hurt as he must be." Trent said.

"We are dealing with the Goddess Hel here. Don't underestimate her." George said. "The sword was gone; he is a big threat."

"We need to let Alastrine know what's going on." Charles added.

"Time is short." Trent said.

"I will send two carrier pigeons to the elf king. That is where Alastrine is going." Paxton said.

"Send three, that's a good magical number." George said.

"Let's hope at least one makes it." Charles said.

MJ laid in her bed and could hear them talking down the hall. She slowly fell asleep.

"Mary Jean." A voice came to her.

She knew the voice but couldn't figure out who it was.

"Mary Jean." The voice came again.

Mary Jean slowly opened her eyes, and she was a girl again playing out front of her house.

"Mary Jean come here please." It was her mother's voice.

"Yes mom." She had gone and sat on the step by her.

"One day I hope you will follow in my footsteps and keep this city growing."

"OK, mom." MJ said still not sure what she was talking about.

"Please remember what I said. I know you will make me proud." She hugged MJ.

* * * *

Hunter looked, as more dark clouds rolled in. It had been raining steady for the last several hours, he swore if Regina said she told him it was going to rain one more time he might hurt her. At least the rain drowned out her voice for the most part.

"You think it will be safe to stop for the night soon. I'm tired and wet and feel like I am going to pass out." Lauren yelled to Hunter. Hunter looked around and could tell the sun was going down even through the dark clouds.

"We will look for a place to stop." Hunter said. Their progress had been slowed; they hadn't covered as much ground as he had hoped. The troll was still out there somewhere. The rain would have covered their tracks making it harder for him to track them, but he also had a shadow helping him, so who knows what he could do.

"This rain is probably going to last all night." Regina said rubbing her hip. Hunter rolled his eyes and looked again for places to stay.

Lauren leaned forward on her horse and almost fell off.

"OK we will stop. There are a few trees just over there." Hunter pointed to the right.

They got to the trees and Tanner got Lauren up next to the tree to help keep as much rain off her as possible. It had been raining so hard the blankets, and everything in their packs were wet. Lauren was shivering and Hunter just hung his head frustrated that he could do nothing to help her right now.

Hunter looked around for something dry to start a fire with and found nothing. Even needles from the pine trees were soaked clean through.

"This storm won't break anytime soon." Regina said as she was finding everything soaked as well.

About twenty minutes later the rain finally let up and soon after stopped. The clouds moved out and the stars came out. Hunter looked at Regina.

"See I told you the storm would break soon." Regina said as she rubbed her shoulder. "My shoulder never lies."

Hunter rolled his eyes and looked out into the darkness. As Regina and Lauren tried to get some sleep. Hunter watched for a while longer and then something in the distance caught his eye. Something had moved in the dark, but Hunter couldn't make it out and couldn't find it again. Hunter was tired and wasn't sure if he was seeing things or not.

"We need to move." Regina was at his side now.

"Why?" Hunter asked already moving.

"Something is wrong. I feel it in my bones." Regina said.

"OK." Hunter was waking Lauren and Regina started getting her stuffed together.

Lauren was slow to move not understanding what was going on. Suddenly Regina grabbed something out of her bag and threw it into the air and a light exploded, and there stood a troll.

"Go!" Hunter yelled.

Regina threw more powder in the troll's face and another explosion happened and the troll screamed in pain.

"Let's go he is temporarily blinded." Regina yelled as they all got on their horses and rode off.

Chapter Twenty-Seven

Lor, Rex, Mir and many other souls and angels were watching the lake of souls. If the Goddess was to make any kind of attack, she would have to come through there.

"I hope the Goddess is going to be alright." One of the souls said as it moves on by.

"She is going to be, ok?" Rex asked the question everyone was thinking.

"She is going to be fine, just needs some rest and positive energy." Came Lofiel's voice.

"So glad you are here." Mir said.

"Any sign of trouble." Lofiel asked.

"No. not yet anyway." Mir said.

"I have gone to Edo in his dreams to try and get him to listen to my dad." Rex said to Lofiel who had told him to do so.

"Any luck in that?"

"I don't think so."

"I was awful when I was alive. I wouldn't listen to me either." Lor sighed.

"Listen many of us are trying to get to those on the other side, to let them know what's going on, with no luck. It seems you two can connect with Edo. Keep trying. I don't know why but she can't block you." Lofiel was putting a positive spin on it.

"Lofiel there is movement in the shadows on her side of the lake."

Lofiel looked to see shadows gathering.

"This is not good." Lofiel said "Get ready to defend our side."

"I was hoping this would not happen." Rex said.

"We all were." Mir added.

* * * * *

The elf king and the others arrived to see the oak trees standing there and all looked confused.

"What has happened here?" The elf king asked.

Everyone looked at Arastrude.

"I'm not sure. The magic that I felt all those years ago came flooding in. I felt the urge to place my palms flat on the ground, and the next thing I knew trees grew." Arastrude said.

"It's the Goddess's magic." Ayre replied.

"You used the protectors magic." Felix pointed to Dagrel seeing his sword.

"How is it you have that sword?" Ryo asked.

Again, they all looked at Arastrude.

"I had a dream that someone was trying to steal the magical items, and I woke up with them in my bed." Arastrude said as she produced the bag with the rest of the items.

"Then that leaves the question of where is Alastrine, doesn't it." Ryo said.

"Things are so out of line right now. I think Luvon, Elyon, Lora and Tanner should have the magical items, just in case the need arises we need them." Ayre said.

Everyone agreed and Arastrude produced their items.

"The Goddess entrusted you with the items, I think you need to hold on to the rest of the items for now." Ryo said.

"I agree with that." Ayre said. "I think we need to head back to the palace now."

They all turned to go, and a big black puff of smoke appeared, and a voice ripped through their minds.

"Give me the items, they are of no use to you."

The magic raced through the six of them.

"Don't try and use the magic on me you mortal fools." The voice talked down to them.

Dagrel and Luvon moved out in front of everyone, Tanner took to the sky. The smoke grew larger and into the sky. Luvon and Tanner shot several arrows into the smoke and laughter filled their head.

"Give them to me now or suffer." The voice was angry now.

Arastrude motioned for Lora and Elyon to do what she was doing. They all put their palms on the ground and asked each of their elements to aid them.

Dagrel, Luvon and Tanner were making another stand to no avail. Then suddenly out of nowhere white clouds blew in around the dark cloud.

"What are you doing?" The voice was confused.

Heavy rain came from the clouds and wrapped around the dark cloud in a spiral squeezing the Darkness.

"What is happening." The voice came again.

Soon a dust storm swirled dirt around the bottom of the dark cloud as the water and wind pushed the dark cloud down into the dust. Then all of the sudden the darkness was gone. Then the clouds pulled the water back and the dirt receded back into the ground.

"What just happened?" Ryo stood in disbelief.

They all looked back at the girls who were pulling their palms off the ground.

Chapter Twenty-Eight

Alastrine was standing outside of the Chapel with two priest and darkness fell.

"What is happening?" The one priest looked at the sky.

"It's only midafternoon." The other chimed in.

"I don't like the look or feel of this. Get inside and lock the doors." Alastrine ordered and he turn to race toward the stairs leading to the plateau.

"It's her, isn't it?" The one priest asked and didn't wait for an answer as they could see the darkness gather into one big mass.

"Everyone inside!" The other priest rushed all those who were staring in shock at what they were seeing. Everyone started running and screaming. The negative energy that was coming from the dark cloud was almost overwhelming.

"Why is she showing herself?" Alastrine mutters as he hit the stairs cloak pulled tight and sword out. "Please my lady be with me."

As he raced up the stairs the wind picked up again and there where white clouds.

"My lady you have returned." Alastrine smiled to himself. Then he felt something that made him stop, something he hadn't felt in many years, and he wasn't sure what it was. He looked up in time to see water swirling around the dark cloud, and then a dust storm. He felt that strange feeling again.

"The stones! But how?" Alastrine moved faster up the stairs now. Soon the black cloud was retreating, and the dust and water went away. Alastrine got to the top of the stairs and was shocked to see oak trees standing there, and off in the distance there was a group of people. A hawk man was in the air using the magic bow shooting arrows into the ground where the dark cloud had gone.

"But how?" Alastrine asked as he raced to where the group stood.

"Are they ok?" Ayre asked as Ryo checked the girls who had all passed out from the use of the magic.

"I believe so. They are breathing fine." Ryo said after checking the last one.

"Someone is coming." Dagrel pointed to a figure running toward them.

Tanner took to the air and Luvon and Dagrel jumped in front of the group to protect everyone.

"It's Alastrine." Tanner yelled back to everyone.

"Thank the Goddess, it's about time." Ayre sighed heavy.

"What happened and how did it happen?" Alastrine asked when he arrived.

"Arastrude woke up with the magical items in bed with her. The elders had told her to come see the elf king." Dagrel started.

"That means Oliver used the sword to break into my house." Alastrine said angerly.

"Who is Oliver and what sword?" Ryo asked.

"He has Lor's sword."

Everyone just looked at each other in disbelief.

ABOUT THE AUTHOR

Donald L Murray Jr. was born in central Pennsylvania. As a senior in high school, Donald wrote his first book, a Hardy boy's style book, that got him an A in English class. Donald spent four years in the Army, where he lived in Germany, as well as being involved in the first gulf war. Since coming home, he moved to northeast Pennsylvania where Donald was involved with community theater for over twelve years as well as taking an improve class in New York City. Donald married his husband, Anthony, and took his last name, Marino. Besides sitting at home writing donald also loves to travel. Donald's favorite author is Terry Brooks.

More book by Donald L. Marino

FANTASY
Return of the Shadows
Book One The Chosen
Book Two Under Attack
Book Three The Final Stand

SHORT STORIES
I was prompted to write these stories.

LOVE STORIES
Carl's Journey

CHILDREN'S BOOKS
Tinsel's First Snow Fall

www.ingramcontent.com/pod-product-compliance
Lightning Source LLC
LaVergne TN
LVHW041709060526
838201LV00043B/650